Cowboy Uncertainty

Cynthia Hickey

The Cowboys of Misty Hollow, Book 5

ISBN-13: 978-1-965352-17-5

Chapter One

Pressley Hamilton glanced at the GPS on her phone. She had to be getting close to the turnoff. Uncle Frank said she'd miss it if she blinked.

A horn blasted to her left.

She shrieked and jerked the steering wheel to the right. Her car skidded toward the steep cliff of Misty Mountain. Not for the first time, she regretted her uncle sending her on this job. But, she wanted to rise in the company, and that meant sometimes doing the more unpleasant things. However, it certainly didn't include dying.

She regained control of the vehicle and glared in her rearview mirror at the dark green truck with a white logo on the tailgate. Imbecile. Noting an area widened for people to park at a scenic lookout, she pulled over and counted to ten until her breathing returned to normal.

That's it. Pressley had always prided herself on maintaining control even in the most stressful situations. Almost careening over the side of a mountain definitely fit into that category. She opened her door and stepped out, her kitten heels crunching the rocks mixed with dirt.

She stepped up on the rock barricade erected to keep onlookers from falling to their death. Just then a slight breeze pulled her scarlet scarf from her head. The silky fabric floated over the valley below. No! She loved that scarf.

Once she recovered, Pressley took in the view before her. The expanse of green, split up by the occasional farm and the town in the distance, took her breath away. What would the valley look like in the morning when the mist, which the town was named for, hovered over everything? She'd have to come see for herself. First, work. She turned and returned to her vehicle.

She froze at the sight of the same green truck that had almost run her off the road. Leaning against the hood, ankles crossed, glared a handsome man in a black Stetson, scuffed cowboy boots, and faded jeans. His intense dark eyes didn't soften as she approached her car. Well, two could play that game. She hiked her chin. "You almost ran me off the road."

"I beg to differ. You weren't watching where you were going. I came back to make sure you hadn't gone over the cliff."

"What if I had? It isn't as if you could go after me." She rolled her eyes.

"I could've called for a helicopter to cart your body out." He pushed away from the truck. "Be more careful, ma'am. You might not be so lucky next time."

Her gaze flicked to the truck logo. Rocking W Ranch. *Good.* she'd complain to his boss once she'd finished her work for the day. "Thank you for your concern, Cowboy."

His lips twitched, and he touched the brim of his

hat. "Welcome." Long strides carried him to the driver's side where he climbed in and drove off with a wave of his hand out the window.

Mercy, the man was gorgeous. If only his attitude was as lovely as his face, and those arms…well, she refused to let her mind go there. *It's been too long, Pressley, since you've been on a date.*

Not wanting a repeat, she studied the GPS before pulling away from the lookoff. The cowboy would probably have known where she needed to turn, but she hadn't thought to ask. No matter. She'd drive up and down the mountain until she found the road.

She wound her hair into a messy bun on top of her head and continued up the mountain looking for the turnoff. The man at the drugstore in town said to look for a tree split in two from lightning. Unfortunately, the GPS didn't show landmarks, and her phone signal kept cutting in and out.

Ah. There was the tree split almost in half, but still alive with lush green leaves. She turned left onto what could in no way be described as a road. Foliage scraped the side of her car. Uncle Frank would have to pay for a new paint job. Or at least Hamilton Enterprises would.

The car bounced its way down the road until it entered a clearing. Instead of towering trees, this area contained saplings and grass as high as the hood of the car.

Pressley frowned. There would certainly be snakes. Why hadn't her uncle told her to dress for snakes? How did one prepare to wander through snake-infested territory anyway? With a groan, she shoved her door open past the thick grass and stepped outside. The car would've scared anything away in the near vicinity, right? She glanced around the ground, finally finding a long stick as thick as her wrist.

Waving it in front of her like a blind person, she moved through the grass and weeds, her scarlet-red heels sinking into the earth. Next time, she'd do a better job of picking her footwear. But, oh, how she loved these shoes.

She huffed when her heel got caught in a weed, then she continued. Uncle Frank wanted a complete report on the condition of the property before making a bid. In her opinion, it would take a lot of funds to clear the land before building, but that's what Hamilton Enterprises did. Clear and build.

After a half an hour of scouting the land, she returned to her car and called her uncle. "It looks worth the money to me, but needs to be bushhogged. Lots of overgrowth."

"Did you see a cave or mine?"

"No, should I have?"

"I've heard there's an old quartz mine on that land. I want to make sure it's boarded up before I send people in there to work. We can't afford any injuries or lawsuits."

She grimaced. "Is it okay if I do that tomorrow? I need to make sure I wear the proper clothes and shoes."

"Of course. I assume you booked a motel room indefinitely?"

"Yes." Not the sort of room she'd grown accustomed to as an adult, but it was clean and the bed mattress fairly new. "I'll come back and look for a mine tomorrow." Hopefully, she wouldn't fall in it while searching. "Anything else?"

"Call me at the end of the day tomorrow. Once a day is sufficient, Pressley. I'm a busy man." Click.

Straight to the point, her uncle.

Pressley looked up the directions to the Rocking W Ranch on her phone. Wonderful. Only a mile up the mountain. The edge of the ranch property abutted the land her uncle wanted. Imagine that.

~

River Swanson rolled out from under one of the trucks used to pull horse trailers and wiped his greasy hands on a rag. He shook his head. Some of the vehicles needed a junkyard rather than maintenance, but as one of the ranch mechanics, he'd do his best.

"Hey, the boss wants you. Some woman is here complaining." Willy grinned from the doorway of the garage. "She's a looker, too."

River shook his head. The reckless driver with the strawberry-blond hair, no doubt. "On my way."

He couldn't remove all the oil from the callouses on his hands or from under his fingernails without a thorough washing, but since the woman was here to complain about something that was clearly her fault, he didn't see the need. He marched for the front porch where his boss, Dylan Wyatt, and the woman stood by the door waiting for him..

"Yeah?"

Dylan glanced his way. "Miss Hamilton says you almost ran her off the mountain."

River turned his attention to the woman. "She's mistaken. I clearly saw her look away from the road and veer into my lane. I honked. Then she swerved."

"Your honk frightened me." She crossed her arms, emerald eyes flashing. "I glanced at my GPS for a split second. You came around that hairpin curve like a bat out of…well, Hades." She hitched her chin. "Deny it."

"I'm denying it." He matched her posture.

Dylan exhaled slowly. "Looks like it's a he said, she said. Since no one is injured, perhaps we could let this go with both parties pledging to be more careful in the future?"

"Perhaps." Miss Hamilton shrugged. "The company I'm working for is looking to purchase the land east of you."

River frowned. "Needs a lot of work. No one has bothered with that property in well over fifty years."

"I saw the extent of the work. The man who employed me says there's an old mine on the property. Is there?"

Dylan turned his attention to River. "I've heard something to that effect, but my twins have roamed all over this mountain and never said anything about a mine."

She crossed her arms. "Would you ask them, please? It would save me a lot of time, Mr. Wyatt."

"Dylan, please. Yes, have a seat. I'll send out our cook with tea." He motioned toward the the round table with four cushioned chairs.

The last thing River wanted was to share tea with this woman. He stifled a groan. "Have a seat, Miss Hamilton. It might be a few minutes."

"Pressley." She sat in one of the chairs, crossing one red-heeled foot over the other. "And you are?"

"River Swanson, ranch mechanic." He sat in the chair next to hers.

"Ah, so you must have been speed testing the truck." A slight smile teased her full lips.

Who was this woman? Prickly one minute, a comedian the next. "Sure." He glanced toward the garage. The truck wouldn't fix itself. Since the boss hadn't dismissed him, he wasn't sure whether he should stay or return to work. He'd just stood to leaveto when Dylan and his twin sons came around the corner of the house. The boss did not look pleased. He sat back down.

"These two said they know the location of the mine." He shot them a look that clearly said they were in trouble. "They will show you the location on Saturday morning. Can you be here by ten ?"

"Absolutely." Pressley smiled. "With doughnuts as payment for their help."

"No, ma'am. These two have been playing where they shouldn't. No reward, please." Dylan shook his head. "They don't seem to have any concept about the danger of playing in abandoned mines."

"It's our clubhouse." Eric glared. "Our *secret* clubhouse. I ain't takin' no woman there."

The boss stooped to his son's level. "You'll do as I say. Now go do your homework before I ground the both of you."

They stomped into the house.

Dylan straightened. "River, I need to attend an auction on Saturday. Since you and Pressley are already acquainted, I'd like you to accompany her and the boys to the mine. Do you mind?"

Yes. "No, sir. I'll be ready." His Saturday was ruined before it began.

Chapter Two

Pressley left her motel the next morning wearing a sundress and sensible shoes. She might not be headed to the land that day, but she didn't see much sense in driving around the small town of Misty Hollow when she could walk. She smiled and waved at passing cars on her way to the diner she'd spotted the day before. The motel's meager continental breakfast didn't seem nearly as appetizing as home-cooked, diner food.

A bell jingled as she opened the diner door and stepped inside. The aromas of freshly brewed coffee and fried doughnuts greeted her. Heads turned from the lunch counter, booths, and tables. Country music played softly from overhead speakers.

"Just one?" A young woman who looked barely out of high school grabbed a menu.

"Just one." Pressley followed her to a small table near the window.

"Coffee?"

"Please, with cream and sugar." She opened the menu, pleased at the inexpensive prices. Uncle Frank had given her an expense account, but the less she spent, the longer she had to find that mine. If she ran out of money, he'd call her back to Memphis.

Oh, chocolate gravy! She hadn't had any since she was a girl. Forget the calories. She could indulge for one day, right? When the hostess returned with her coffee, she gave her the order.

The girl, *Holly*, her nametag read, smiled. "I'll pass that on to your server."

A few minutes later, a woman with Lucille Ball red hair teased into an impressive beehive brought Pressley her breakfast. "Howdy. I'm Lucy. You passing through?" She set the plate with two biscuits slathered with melted butter and a ton of chocolate gravy in front of Pressley.

"I'm here on business. This looks delicious." She took a big sniff.

"One of our favorite dishes. Welcome to Misty Hollow. Let me know if I can bring you anything else or answer any of your questions about our town." She turned to go.

"I do have a question if you have the time."

"Of course. Shall I sit?"

"Sure." Pressley motioned to the seat across from her. "I'm here looking at land for the company I work for, Hamilton Enterprises out of Memphis, and since I've arrived in Misty Hollow, I've heard there is an old mine on the land we're interested in." She cut into a biscuit.

Lucy sighed. "The old Duncan place. No one has cared about that mine for over fifty years. Why now?"

"It wasn't the mine I was sent here to look at." Lines creased the woman's forehead. Why did the woman look worried?

"There's a fallen-down shack up there

somewhere. You find it, you should find the mine." Lucy crossed her arms. "What do you want to know?"

"Someone's showing me the mine tomorrow." Pressley tilted her head. "What's bothering you?"

Lucy folded her hands and leaned forward. "That place is haunted, some say. Bad luck. There's a story there."

"I'm listening." Her hand holding the fork paused halfway to her mouth. Anticipation coursed through her. "I love old stories."

"This one dates back a hundred years or more. Back when the mine caved in, burying a young man alive. His betrothed tried to dig him out, causing another cave-in. She perished. Some folks say you can hear her cries to this day."

"How horrible." Pressley put a hand to her heart. She'd heard stories of people loving someone so much they'd die for them. Unfortunately, she'd never met anyone she could say the same of. "You can hear the cries today?"

"Well—" Lucy shrugged. "No one has been up there for a long time. The mine has tape around it warning folks to stay away. I'm guessing you have permission from the Duncan family?"

Pressley nodded. "The company does. Why did no one dig those poor people out?"

"Ghosts." Lucy laughed. "Oh, today, we have more sense…mostly. It's danger that keeps most people away. If your company purchases that land, I'd advise you to close off that mine for good."

"Is there still quartz in there?"

"No idea." Lucy slid from the booth. "A word of caution, ma'am. This town holds tight to its urban legends. Most folks won't take kindly to you nosing around up there."

"I'm not nosing. We are purchasing that land."

"I'm just warning you, is all. Don't take offense if some folks have harsh words with you."

"What do *you* believe?"

Lucy paled. "I believe what my father did. That there is still quartz in that mine, and someday, someone would come for it and not let anything stand in their way."

Pressley almost choked on her biscuit. "That isn't our way. We're developers."

"Folks won't like that either." Lucy headed for the kitchen.

An elderly man in denim overalls leaned over the booth behind Pressley. His coffee-scented breath wafted over her. "Something evil stalks that place, Miss. It's been sleeping for a long time. Why do you want to come and wake it up?"

"I don't believe in ghosts, sir." She glanced up. "If there is something going on at that mine, it's most likely kids. In fact, it's the Wyatt twins who are showing me where it's located. They said it's their secret clubhouse."

"Those young'uns weren't alive fifty years ago when this all started. Watch your back, Miss. There are things deep in that ground best left alone." He slid from the booth and shuffled to the cash register.

Rather than be frightened, Pressley found herself more intrigued than ever and couldn't wait to set foot in the mine. Since the Wyatt twins were still alive, the place must have settled over the years, filling in places that could cave.

She finished her breakfast, tossed a tip on the table, then paid for her meal. Curious eyes followed her out the door. When she glanced back from the sidewalk, several people watched her through the window which creeped her out far more than any make-believe ghost could.

From everything she'd read on the internet, Misty Hollow was supposed to be a friendly, welcoming town. The glares tossed her way said otherwise.

Her phone rang. "Good morning, Uncle Frank."

"Plans for today?"

"Nothing. I don't have a guide to the mine until tomorrow, remember?" She shook her head at the impatient tone in his voice. "Although, the residents here don't seem pleased that we're purchasing that land, or that I'm headed to the mine tomorrow."

"We don't care what they think. Once that housing development is built, they'll come to their senses."

She didn't think so. Most small towns were reluctant to change. "Is there something you wanted me to do before tomorrow?"

"Keep feeling out the town, I guess. I need to know the opposition." Click.

Strange request. The purchase was a done deal as far as she knew. The Duncan family seemed more than happy to sell the land at the one-million-dollar price her uncle offered them.

She stopped on the sidewalk and glanced both ways in search of something to help fill the hours before the next day. The sign for a bookstore beckoned her, and she headed that way.

A few minutes later, clutching a bag that

contained two romantic comedies and a couple of thrillers, she exited the bookstore. Two women stared and whispered her way before turning up their noses and heading in the opposite direction.

Time would move very slowly if everyone looked at Pressley as something stuck on the bottom of their shoe. She heaved a sigh and headed for the corner drugstore.

~

River exited the mercantile in time to see Pressley enter the drugstore. The mercantile owner, Fred Murphy, had filled him in on how the folks of Misty Hollow felt about the business with the mine. River didn't have an opinion one way or the other.

He'd come to Misty Hollow to work, to heal after the battles he'd fought in the Middle East, not to worry about ghosts. The only ghosts that haunted him were in his mind. He frowned as Pressley left the drugstore empty-handed. Her pretty face fell. With a groan, River headed her way. "What happened?"

"That man refused to let me purchase anything. Said he didn't want troublemakers in town." Her eyes shimmered. "I've never been treated this way before."

"Come on." River took her by the elbow and led her back into the store. "Grab the things you need." He refused to let anyone treat a woman that way.

"Now, look here, River. If the folks of this town don't wait on this woman, she'll leave that mine in peace." Orson Heath crossed his arms and glared over River's shoulder.

"If not her, then someone else. Be a good man and add up her purchases." River frowned. "She's only doing her job."

Pressley set a few toiletries on the counter and backed up a few steps.

Orson scowled and rang them up. "A man has a right to his opinion," he murmured.

"And a woman has a right to do the job she's hired to do," River said. "She isn't the one responsible here."

"All you cowboys at that ranch are always sticking your noses in other people's business."

"Only when there's a wrong being done. Thank you, Orson. Pressley." He handed her the bag, then with his hand on the small of her back he guided her from the store. "Sorry you had to experience that. Sometimes these people can be small-minded. Give them time. They'll come around."

"I won't be here long enough. Thank you for your help. See you tomorrow." She clutched her bags and headed for the motel.

"Hey, River." Deputy Hudson stopped his squad car next to River's truck. "Nice day."

"Yep." He moved to the driver's side.

"Heard about some hassling of a newcomer?"

River told the deputy about the purchasing of the Duncan place.

Hudson shook his head. "It never ceases to amaze me how many people believe in ghosts and evil spirits. The only evil I've ever encountered came from humans."

"You and me both." War had taught him enough about evil. "Once the purchase is complete, she'll move on, and these folks can direct their anger at the new owner."

"Agreed. Let me know if the trouble gets worse

than words and dirty looks." Hudson drove away.

River stared after him. Why would the deputy ask that? River wasn't responsible for Pressley, nor did he want to be. He climbed into the driver's seat of his truck, drove to the motel to make sure Pressley made it safely there, then headed home. Not because he cared, but because it's what a cowboy…a gentleman did. Especially when folks resented her presence in their town. Darn it. Now, he'd be keeping an eye on her for as long as she stayed in Misty Hollow.

All he could do was hope it wasn't for long.

Chapter Three

Not wanting to face the disapproving glares of the Misty Hollow residents, Pressley ordered leather coverings for her legs and had them delivered to the motel. Now, she stood in front of the full-length mirror on the back of the bathroom door and laughed.

They were meant to protect a person from snake bites, but they looked silly over her jeans, and even worse when she'd put them on wearing shorts. Oh, well. Better to be silly-looking than bitten and dead. She slung her camera case over her shoulder, grabbed her purse and the keys to the rental car, and strolled out the door.

The motel manager who was sweeping the sidewalk turned to her with wide eyes. "Uh, good morning?"

"Good morning." She grinned and got into her car. The poor man stared as she drove away. No doubt those on the ranch would look at her the same way when she arrived.

The twins met her as soon as she slid out of her car. They blinked like a couple of owls before one of them said, "Are you trying to be a cowboy? Where's your hat and horse? That's the only time anyone wears chaps."

"These are to protect me from snake bites." She pasted on a smile.

"Noise will do that," the other boy said before yelling through the screen door that "the woman" was here.

River stepped onto the porch, took one look at her, and spewed his coffee. "Sorry." He swiped the back of his hand across his mouth.

"Are we ready?"

He cleared his throat. "Would you like a cup of coffee first? The boys said it's quite a hike to the mine."

"We aren't driving?"

"Nope."

"Well, then, yes, please." She followed him into the house.

Several cowboys glanced her way, then grinned. None of them said anything other than howdy, but they didn't need to. The amusement on their faces said it all.

She accepted a cup of coffee from a woman in a ruffled yellow apron and took a seat at the table. "I guess no one here is afraid of snakes."

"Sure, we are," the cook said, patting her on the back. "We're just used to them is all. Don't mind this bunch. You do what makes you feel safe."

"Thank you. I'm Pressley Hamilton."

"Mrs. White is what these scoundrels call me. Nice to meet you. I'll be sending along a sack lunch for the four of you and some bottles of water. Be ready in a jiffy."

By the time Pressley finished her coffee and

answered a ton of questions from the cowboys around the table, Mrs. White handed River a large floral backpack. "Don't mind the bag. It's the only one not being used right now."

He held the pack by two fingers as if it would bite him. "Flowers?"

"Oh, hush. You're man enough to carry it off. See you later and be careful." She aimed the last sentence at the twins.

"We will." They said in unison as they dashed out the door.

River exhaled heavily. "Ready?"

"Yes." Pressley grinned. "Want me to carry the backpack?"

"I do not." He waved for her to go ahead of him. "If you can wear that, then I can carry this."

The boys, accompanied by a large mixed-breed dog named Monster, led them across the wide expanse of cleared land between the main house and the woods rising behind it. They complained all the way about having to show a girl where their secret clubhouse was and how her buying it would ruin everything.

"What's the story about the mine being haunted?" Ignoring their complaints, she fell into step next to River.

"I don't know much since I've only lived here about a year. The person you want to talk to is June Whatley. She knows everything about everybody around these parts, but best I can recall is that a couple died a very long time ago." He hitched the backpack more firmly on his shoulders.

"I know that part. Why are people so upset that I'm scouting out the mine?" There had to be more to the story. "I'm looking for history."

"Why?" His brow furrowed.

"An interesting history is a good selling point." She shrugged. "The doomed lovers is nice, but there has to be more."

"We found a box of old letters and a book." One of the twins glanced over his shoulder at them.

"That's great." Pressley grinned. "How do I tell them apart?"

"Eric's hair is a tad darker, and he has a freckle on his upper lip. He's also more talkative than Derrick."

"That should help." If she was looking at their faces. "How much farther?"

"We should reach the edge of the property in a few minutes. As for the mine, I don't know."

"There should be a shack close by."

"I've not had any reason to come out this way."

The man was literally no help. As the foliage thickened around them, she started searching the ground for snakes.

"The dog will scare away any snakes," River said.

"I'm not taking any chances."

"You don't like giving up control, do you?"

"No, I don't." He'd figured her out fast enough. She definitely liked being in control of every aspect of her life. Including looking out for snakes.

A half an hour later, the twins picked up speed.

"Hold on, boys." River did the same, leaving Pressley no alternative but to barge through the tall grass and weeds after them.

They ran past a fallen cabin built of logs and toward a hill. The boys soon disappeared out of sight.

Pressley stopped to catch her breath. "Where did

they go?"

"The mine opening must be here somewhere." River shoved aside some low-hanging branches, revealing a crevice between what looked like two large stones but were actually the walls of the mine. "Be careful." He pulled a small flashlight from his pocket and shined it inside. "Boys?"

"We're here."

The temperature inside dropped at least twenty degrees from the summer heat outside. Pressley rubbed her hands down her arms and studied her surroundings. Damp walls of dirt and stone. In front of them a tunnel beckoned.

"Here's the box of stuff." Derrick handed it to her. "We found it a long ways down there." He pointed to the tunnel. "But, then dirt started to fall on our heads, so we haven't gone back."

"That was a very smart decision." She glanced into the box. Not only letters tied with decaying ribbon but also yellowed newspapers and a cracked leather journal.

~

"Let's stop for lunch before exploring further." River shrugged out of the backpack and pulled out sandwiches, apples, and bottles of water.

"Thanks." Pressley barely glanced up from the box as she took her lunch, instead she carried it all to a stump someone had dragged into the mine and sat. "This should tell me a lot about the history of this place."

"Should you take it out of here?" River frowned. "It doesn't belong to you or your employer yet."

"I won't keep it, and I'll turn it into whatever

historical society Misty Hollow has." She unwrapped her sandwich, excitement coursing through her. "This is quite the find, boys."

"It's just a bunch of paper. We were going to give it to Dad." Eric took a bite out of his apple. "But, the last time we were here, we heard some weird things coming from down the tunnel. It scared us, so we left."

River jerked his attention away from his food. "What kind of weird things?"

"Sounds." Derrick glanced behind him.

"Moaning, banging…you know." Eric took a bite of his apple. "Ghost noises."

"There's no such things as ghosts." River stared at the tunnel.

"I'm just saying what we heard."

Pressley's eyes glittered in the dimness of the mine. "Should we check it out? What if someone is trapped down there?"

"After we eat. The boys will stay here." The boss would have his head if anything happened to the boys. If someone was trapped down there, River would get help for them without involving the twins. When he'd finished eating, he asked Pressley to stay with the boys, not surprised when she refused, then led the way down the tunnel, the flashlight not providing as much light as he'd like. He doubted anyone was trapped, and he seriously questioned whether the boys had actually heard anything. Still, it had to be checked out. Just in case.

"Do you think we'll find anything?" Pressley whispered.

"No, and no need to whisper. It's only us here."

"Right, but this place is creepy. Can't you hear the

timbers creaking?"

He glanced overhead, praying none of them would fall. If the slightest bit of dust coated his head, he'd turn back immediately. "You might as well see all you can about the property before your company purchases it."

"Right." She lifted her camera and snapped some photos. The flash illuminated the area better than his flashlight could.

Spotting something shiny, River aimed the light to his left. "There's still quartz in this mine." So, why wasn't it being mined?

"My uncle was under the impression the mine was mined out."

"Or he wants you to think that."

Her eyes widened. "Why would he lie?"

"To get the land for less money." He shrugged. "Folks have lied for less."

"He wouldn't do that." She spit the words through gritted teeth. "The land is practically already his. We're waiting for the last family member to sign."

"Why haven't they?"

"They haven't responded to our communication in the last couple of weeks. One of my jobs here in Misty Hollow is to locate that person."

River shined the light over the rest of the walls. "He lives here?"

"To my knowledge."

"Hmm." Not finding anything else, he continued down the tunnel. "Maybe this person doesn't want to sign."

"Then I'll convince him to, and it's a he. A Roger Duncan."

"Don't know the man."

"Well, somebody in this town does."

"Good luck."

She huffed. "Are you like the other people in this town—resentful of my being here? I'm simply doing my job. Once that's accomplished, I'll be gone."

"No, ma'am. Your being here doesn't affect me in any other way than the fact you're keeping me from my work by my having to guide you here."

"Let me assure you that in the future, your guidance will no longer be needed. I can find my own way."

She sure was a spitfire. He bit back a grin, taking more enjoyment out of riling her than he should.

A moan sounded from above them.

The hair on the back of his neck stood.

Pressley clutched his arm. "What was that?"

"Timbers shifting?"

"It sounded human."

"Hello? Anybody here?" River shined the light above their heads.

A woman screamed. Not like any scream he'd ever heard before; more like the caterwaul of a cougar he'd once seen trapped. Where could a cat of that size hide in here?

"Let's go."

"But what is it?" Her hold tightened.

"A cougar, maybe. We need to get back to the boys." He took her hand and led her back to the mine entrance where the twins waited near the opening.

"I told you," Eric said.

"It's a mountain lion. Nothing more."

"Then where's the scat? You know...the poop."

The boy crossed his arms. "Or growl? And why didn't it try to eat us?"

The boy had more questions than River had answers. Maybe he should accompany Pressley again, just to see what he could find out.

Chapter Four

Pressley opened her eyes to the sound of scratching at her motel-room door. Since the room's doors were all on the outside, she guessed it could be a stray animal, until it moaned like someone in pain.

She tossed aside the thin sheet she'd covered up with and padded to the door to peek out the peephole. Not seeing anything, she moved to the window and peered through a slit in the curtains. Still nothing.

Could there be rats in the walls? That would explain the scratching but not the moaning. She stilled and listened. Nothing. A nervous chuckle escaped her. The sounds had been nothing more than leftover imaginings from being in the mine the day before. She shuddered. She'd be returning there in a few hours with a stronger flashlight to take a closer look. Alone.

Would River go with her if she asked? The man had said she'd kept him from his work. Would the ranch owner lend her someone else? It wouldn't hurt to stop by and ask.

After a quick shower, she dressed in dark skinny jeans, her snake leather, ankle boots, and a short-sleeve tee shirt. She wouldn't spare a second thought at how others looked at her. Safety was her top priority.

On second thought, she did care how about how she looked. Pressley removed the snake-leather coverings. She'd put them on after her breakfast at the diner.

Opening her room door, she stuck her head out and glanced both ways. No sign of anyone, two-legged or four. The sounds that had awakened her had to be nothing more than her imagination.

She slowed as she approached her car. A sheet of white paper flapped from under the windshield wiper. Her hands trembled as she freed it and read, *Trouble comes to those who venture into the mine. Stay away.*

Her eyes did a slow scan around the area before unlocking her car and tossing the warning note inside. She contemplated taking it to the police, but the computer-printed, block lettering wouldn't give them a clue as to who had left it. Most likely it was from one of the disgruntled town residents who had glared at her after hearing about her purpose for being in town.

Nasty looks shot her way when she entered the diner, making her wish for a fast-food place to pick up a meal on the go. But, since Misty Hollow didn't have one, she sighed, squared her shoulders, and followed the hostess to the same booth she'd sat in the day before.

Pressley glanced at the day's breakfast special of ham-and-cheese omelet. "I'll have the special, orange juice, and coffee, please."

"Yes, ma'am." The young girl smiled and headed for the kitchen.

Pressley shrugged. Only the older folks seemed to

resent her presence. She folded her hands in her lap and stared out the window as dawn announced the new day.

A sheriff's department car cruised slowly past. People smiled and waved. Women holding firmly to the hands of small children strolled down the sidewalk and in and out of shops opening for the day. A picture reminiscent of a Norman Rockwell painting except for the glares still being tossed her way.

Maybe the diner made meals to go. It would be a hassle to pick up her meals and take them back to her room, but it would be better than this.

"Here you go, ma'am. Enjoy." The server set her order in front of her. "Oh, your coffee." She rushed away, returning a moment later with a carafe and a cup. "I'm sorry. I'm new and not used to the morning rush."

"New to town or to the job?" Pressley smiled up at her.

"The job. I've lived here my whole life."

"Do you know anything about the old Duncan mine?"

"Only that it's dangerous." A question flickered in her eyes as she lowered her voice. "And that folks around here don't like you poking around."

"Why not? That old urban legend happened a long time ago, if it was ever real in the first place."

"There are secrets that shouldn't be told in these mountains, ma'am. Be careful." She moved to the next table.

Secrets? Every town had secrets. She dug into her omelet, finished as quickly as possible, hurried out after paying, and climbed into her car.

Her phone rang. It was the motel manager asking her to return to the motel as soon as possible. The day was not starting out as she'd planned, and Pressley really liked for things to go as planned. Instead of turning right out of the diner parking lot, she went left.

Blinking red and blue lights from a sheriff's department squad car greeted her. Two men in deputy uniforms stood outside her motel room with the manager.

Pressley's heart leaped to her throat. As she pulled into the nearest parking spot, she could see her room door ajar.

"Miss Hamilton?" A deputy wearing a tag that identified him as Hudson greeted her as she climbed from her vehicle.

"Yes?"

"It appears as if there's been a break-in. We'd like you to take a look and let us know whether anything is missing."

"Someone broke into my room?" Her mouth dropped open.

"It appears that way. The manager noted the door open and called the department."

Pressley stepped into chaos. Bedding puddled on the floor, drawers left open, her makeup bag scattered across the bathroom counter. "At first glance, there's nothing missing. I don't have much and definitely not anything someone would want to…"

"What?" His eyes narrowed.

"Nothing. I have nothing." Except for a box of papers in the trunk of her car. A box she wasn't ready to hand over to the authorities. "Except for a note." She rushed back to her car and retrieved the sheet of paper. "I found this on my car this morning."

His features hardened as he read the note. "You

didn't think you should give us a call, Miss Hamilton?"

"No." She shook her head. "The people of this town made it very clear how they felt about my company purchasing the Duncan land. I merely thought one of them left the note."

"One of them most likely did, but the ransacking of your room is a crime. Please be careful, Miss Hamilton. We'll look into this."

She nodded and watched as he climbed into his car, followed by the other deputy. She sighed and went to straighten her room. Fortunately, the manager promised to change the lock to something sturdier.

Sirens drew her back to the door. The deputy's car made a U-turn and sped in the opposite direction.

~

River pulled over as the flashing lights appeared in his rearview mirror, then pulled out behind the speeding squad car and followed it. Dread sat like a rock in his stomach. Although he had a truck bed full of feed and a delivery he'd promised to drop off to an elderly farmer on the edge of town, he feared the worst.

The deputy's car passed old man Rupert's place. Still River followed, his curiosity piqued. It wouldn't be the first time the sheriff's office had called on the help of the cowboys of the Rocking W Ranch, and he wanted to make himself available in case they needed him.

River followed up a long drive to a house he wasn't familiar with. He tapped his horn and rolled down his window. "I'll stay out here unless you need me," he called out to Hudson.

"Good to know." Hudson approached the house where a man in faded green coveralls awaited him.

River couldn't hear what was being said, but it was obvious from the man's gestures he was agitated. A few minutes later, the two deputies entered the house. When they came back out, Hudson marched toward River's truck. He opened the door and got out. "What is it?"

"Do you know a Roger Duncan?"

He frowned. "No, should I?"

"Maybe not, but that Miss Hamilton is here to look at the Duncan land, and you were with her yesterday. She say anything about meeting up with him?"

He shrugged. "She did say she was going to look him up. He's the last surviving Duncan family member, and the company she works for needs his signature in order to move forward."

"Not anymore. The man's dead." The man in overalls shook his head.

River frowned. "You think Pressley had something to do with it?"

"Not really, but she's mixed up somehow. Her motel room was ransacked this morning. Would you have any idea why?"

"We were up at the mine yesterday. The Wyatt twins handed over a box of old letters and newspapers they'd found. That might be what someone was looking for, but why kill Duncan?"

"That's what I need to find out. Can you get that box from Miss Hamilton and take it to the office? I'd appreciate it, then I can handle things here."

"So, by dead, you mean the man has been murdered?"

"A bullet between the eyes while he sat eating his

breakfast leads me to believe that, yes. If you hurry, you might catch her at her motel room." Hudson turned and returned to the crime scene.

River would do whatever he could to help, but becoming more involved in the mystery surrounding the Duncan mine hadn't been on his radar. He climbed into the driver's seat of his truck and drove to the motel.

Not seeing Pressley's rental car, he drove slowly down Main Street. If he didn't find her there, he'd head up to the mine after dropping off the feed at the ranch. He spotted her on the sidewalk outside the bookstore and pulled up in front of her car. "Pressley."

She set the box from the mine in the trunk of her car. "Good morning. Well, it's almost afternoon now."

"I'm glad to see you have the box. Roger Duncan was found murdered this morning, and the sheriff's department wants the letters and papers."

Her brow lowered. "Murdered? I don't see how these papers will help."

"Obviously, they will. Want me to take them?"

She exhaled heavily and retrieved the box. "Here." She shoved it at him.

"Why did you take it in the bookstore?"

She hitched her chin in what looked like a dare. "I made copies."

"Why?" He frowned.

"I want to know what's going on around here. Tomorrow, I'm going to speak to June Whatley. Somebody tore up my room. Obviously, there is something going on that I need to know about, and Hamilton Enterprises needs to know about." Her features softened. "I feel bad about Mr. Duncan. Not sure what my uncle will do now. I'm sure the purchase will move forward, eventually. All the papers are drawn up." She slammed her trunk closed. "If you'll excuse me, I need to make a phone call."

"May I make a request?"

"Sure." She peered up at him, worry in those remarkable eyes.

"Don't go to the mine alone. Come by the ranch and get me."

"I thought you were busy."

"I am, but I'd rather not find out you suffered the same fate as Roger Duncan." Because she was a human being, a pretty woman—the same request he'd make for anyone. Right. Because everyone looked adorable in leather chaps over stylish jeans, or tottered around on ridiculous, high heels while walking on a ranch, or…he could go on with many reasons why this woman captivated him.

"All right, River. I won't go to the mine without you." Her lips curled in a smile. "How about the day after tomorrow? Ten o'clock. I'll come to the ranch."

"I'll be there." He nodded and set the box in the bed of his truck while his mind tried to come up with a way to ask the boss for time off to help a city girl stir up trouble. Because that's what she was doing. His gut told him that her arrival was bringing in one heck of a storm to Misty Hollow.

Chapter Five

After the break-in, Pressley had moved to a second-floor room. Not that it would prevent anyone from breaking down the door, but it made her feel marginally better. Now, she prepared herself for a visit with June Whatley who had agreed to meet with her.

Would she still be pleased when she found out why? Most of the town still treated Pressley with frosty looks.

She eyed her red heels. "Sorry, girls. This town doesn't seem to be the place to wear you. Hold tight until we return to Memphis." Her phone rang. Uncle Frank. She sighed and answered. "Yes, sir?"

"What is going on? I heard Roger Duncan was found dead."

"Yes."

"This could not happen at a worse time."

"I don't think he chose to be murdered, Uncle Frank. There is more going on here than you or I imagined. I'm going to visit with an old woman who supposedly knows everything about everyone in this town. Maybe she can shed some light on what is happening."

"While you do that, I'll be in a meeting with the lawyers. Try calling me for a change, would you?" Click.

If he gave her a chance, she might call him first. She grabbed her purse and peered out the door to make sure the coast was clear. Not once had she envisioned that coming to Misty Hollow to look at a parcel of land could be dangerous.

She retrieved the photocopied pages and journal from the drawer of the room's nightstand. No way would she leave them behind. Taking a deep breath, she opened the door and hurried down the stairs to her car. Pressley didn't breathe easy until she pulled from the parking lot and drove the short distance to the address June had given her. The woman lived in a two-story Victorian with turrets and a wraparound porch—the sort of house Pressley had always dreamed of owning. She parked next to the curb and exited her car.

An elderly woman with stooped shoulders greeted her before she reached the porch. "Miss Hamilton?"

"Please call me Pressley." She thrust out her hand. "You must be Ms. June Whatley."

"Call me June, and yes, that's me. I've oatmeal cookies and lemonade inside. Coffee if you'd prefer."

"Coffee, please." Since she'd skipped breakfast, the cookies sounded marvelous.

June entered the door first and led Pressley to a small breakfast cove in a clean but outdated kitchen. "Sit, and help yourself. Coffee coming right up."

"Do you know why I'm here?" Pressley sat and put her purse on the chair next to her.

"Sure, I do. Word spreads in this town."

"And you're still willing to answer my questions?"

"Absolutely." She flashed a grin over her shoulder. "It ain't your fault these folks are superstitious or don't like change. Not that I enjoy change either, but I like to think that, despite rarely leaving my house, I'm a little more hip than that."

Pressley bit her lip and ducked her head to prevent the woman from seeing her amusement. She hadn't been here five minutes yet and already loved June Whatley.

"Now—" June set a cup and a tray containing cream and sugar in front of her. "What's all this business about you poking around the Duncan mine?"

"I work for Hamilton Enterprises. My uncle owns the business, and is…was…in negotiations with the Duncan family—"

"The recently deceased Roger Duncan."

"Yes. Anyway, I was sent here to see what condition the land was in and to find the elusive Mr. Duncan so he could sign the closing papers." She stirred cream and sugar into her coffee. "I had no idea there was a quartz mine on that land."

"Some say the place is haunted." June's lips twitched.

"We did hear some rather frightening noises there."

"Who is we?"

"River Swanson and the Wyatt twins who showed me the mine."

"What did you think about River?" Her eyes twinkled.

She didn't see how River was germane to the

visit, but she'd humor the woman. "He's bossy, yet chivalrous—"

"Handsome?" June quirked a brow.

"Yes, he is very handsome." Pressley tilted her head. "Why?"

"Because every time a pretty woman comes to town, trouble and romance follow."

"I am not here for romance." Absolutely not. "I'm here to do a job and nothing more. The sooner I complete that job the better." She sipped her coffee.

"Whatever you say, dear." June nibbled on a cookie. "Ask your questions."

Pressley reached for a cookie. "What can you tell me about that land and mine?"

"It's been there longer than this town for one. The land's been in the Duncan family for a very long time. Until now. Roger was the last of the clan and had no children. He never married. As the story goes…the Duncan family got their hands on the land by winning a poker game back in the late 1800s." She dunked her cookie in her coffee.

Pressley pulled a notebook from her purse and started taking notes.

"The original owner, McGee—I think the name was—wanted the land back and killed the winner of the deed. Then, that Duncan's brother killed McGee. The Duncan brother's lineage goes way back. So, from day one blood has tainted that mine."

"I heard there was a cave-in, and a man and woman died?"

"That's an urban legend with no basis in fact, but it is romantic." June smiled. "Roger Duncan, bless his heart, was diagnosed with prostate cancer a few months ago. Stage four. No doubt that's why he's selling the land."

"Was the mine profitable?"

"Back in the day, yes. Some say it isn't mined out yet."

Pressley kept the news of River's find to herself. "So, that's why it hasn't been permanently closed down."

"Most likely." June's smile faded. "I do need to give you a word of caution, Pressley. You aren't the first to go nosing around that place. Others have offered to buy that land, and all have ended up dead."

A chill ran down her spine. "If there are no more Duncans, who would be against the land being sold?"

"That's the big question, isn't it? Who is willing to resort to murder to keep that land in the Duncan family? I see the gleam in your eye, young lady, and I advise you against trying to solve the mystery."

"It's my job to solve it. That's what I was sent here to do. Find out all I can about that land." Armed with the information she now had, she had to believe that her uncle had already heard a lot of this news and wanted her to separate fact from fiction.

"Well, I'm against it, but I'm just a nosy old woman. You come again, you hear? Anytime you have questions or simply want to talk. It gets lonely here sometimes."

"Why don't you go out?" Pressley stood and returned her notebook to her purse before slinging it over her shoulder.

"My nephew picks me up for church and shopping. If he can't take me where I need to go, I stay here. It's too dangerous out there, Pressley. My gut tells me you're about to find out just how dangerous."

~

While River worked on the axle of a truck, his mind kept going back to the sounds at the mine. On one hand, they sounded human; on the other they sounded like an animal. But neither sounded natural. After supper, he saddled a horse, grabbed his rifle, and then headed for the Duncan land. He wouldn't be able to rest until he found out what had made those noises.

"Where you going?" Eric popped up from behind the barn.

"The Duncan mine."

"Can I go?"

"No, you stay here. If I'm not back by your bedtime, you tell your dad."

Eric frowned. "It's summer. I don't have a bedtime."

"Okay, if I'm not back by nine o'clock. I'm counting on you to have my back." River tugged his hat more firmly on his head, slung his rifle over his shoulder, and gave the boy a nod.

"Got it. I'm going to tell Derrick." He darted into the barn.

The boys would take their job seriously. Not that River expected to meet with harm, but it was always best to stay safe.

The early evening horseback ride soothed his thoughts even as they often turned to Pressley. Would she return to wherever she'd lived if things grew ugly?

He'd asked a few questions of his own around town about the Duncan mine and found out bits and pieces of its cursed history. River didn't believe in ghosts. A live person had to be behind the tragedies that occurred at the mine. Thus, the reason the sounds they'd heard nagged at him.

It chilled his blood to think an evil person could be trying to keep folks away from the mine after discovering the Wyatt twins played there on a regular basis. Obviously, they weren't considered a threat. That also told River it wasn't an animal behind the noises.

Outside the mine, he tethered the horse to a tree near grass, pulled a large flashlight and his rifle from behind the saddle, and pushed aside the foliage covering the mine entrance. Just inside, he let his eyes adjust, then flicked on the flashlight. No screams or moans greeted him.

He swept the flashlight beam across the floor. No new footprints, human or otherwise. No one had been there since Pressley and he had come with the boys. He headed down the tunnel, sweeping the light over every inch of the floor and walls.

A scream almost made him jump out of his skin. Then, a moan.

River turned slowly, running the light along where the rafters kept the roof from caving in. His eyes narrowed. A rock the size of his fist rested between two beams. He stretched as far as he could until he could reach it and pull it down.

River stared at the almost imperceptible light. A motion-detected speaker. That's why they only heard the noises in the tunnel. Someone had to trigger the speaker. He stared into the darkness to his left. What was so important down there that someone would need to scare folks away?

Returning his attention to the rafters over his head, he wrapped his fist around the speaker.

Everything in him wanted to search further. Wisdom held him back. Until the mine was deemed safe, it could be fatal to go deeper. Not to mention the fact the mine did not belong to him, and he could be accused of trespassing.

Who was in charge now that Roger Duncan was dead? Since Pressley had come looking for him, he must have an executor—someone who handled the legalities. Would that person give permission for the mine to be searched?

River would take the speaker to the sheriff and let them handle things. He shouldn't have to worry about Pressley since she had no need to be at the mine until Duncan's affairs were in order and the final paperwork done.

As he stepped from the mine, a shot rang out, kicking a chunk of rock inches from his head. River dove, his hand going to his cheek. His fingers came away bloody. He brought his rifle around and peered through the growing dusk for his assailant.

His horse snorted and pulled at his tether.

"Hush, girl." River belly crawled through the brush.

After several minutes of silence, he picked up a stick and tossed it a few feet away. When no other gunshots rang out, he climbed slowly to his feet.

Someone really didn't want people nosing around the mine.

Chapter Six

Pressley stepped up to the counter in Lucy's. "Pick up for Hamilton."

"Be right up." The server smiled, poured coffee for a gentleman next to Pressley, then headed for the kitchen.

Leaning against the counter, Pressley turned to meet the stares of the townsfolk. She refused to let them intimidate her as she ordered her meal to go.

River, seated at a far corner booth, spotted her and waved for her to join him. Was he serious? Already several heads had turned to shoot glares his way.

"Here you go, ma'am." The server set a Styrofoam box on the counter.

"Am I able to eat this here? I see someone I know."

"Sure. I'll bring you a plate and utensils."

Pressley carried her breakfast to River's table. "You're a brave man, eating with a pariah. What happened to your face?" A bandage covered his left cheek.

"Sit down and I'll tell you."

"Okay, I'm intrigued." She sat across from him, thanking the server when she brought her dishes.

He leaned forward. "I went to the mine last night to investigate what had made those sounds we heard. In the cave, I found a motion-activated speaker." He set what looked like a rock on the table.

She dropped her fork into her country gravy. "No animal?"

"No. When I left the mine, someone shot at me." He put a hand to his face.

"They shot you?" She glanced around, then lowered her voice. "Are you okay?"

"Rock fragment that ricocheted. I didn't even need stitches, although I will have a slight scar."

"It'll make you look daring." She grinned even though her heart rate increased to the point it would burst free.

"I've got enough scars, thank you." He sat back and crossed his arms. "Find anything in the papers?"

"I thought you turned them over to the sheriff." She concentrated on transferring her food to her plate.

"You told me you made copies when I caught you coming out of the bookstore."

She sighed. "Guilty, and I'm slowly making progress. There is a lot of history in this town, and it doesn't all have to do with the mine. It's going to take a while to comb through it all."

"What about the journal?"

"The handwriting is so awful it is going to take even longer." Her shoulders slumped. "What about the speaker rock?"

"I'm taking it to the sheriff when I finish breakfast. Want to tag along? This all concerns you."

"Does it?" She could see the land purchase trickling through her uncle's fingers.

"Yes. Your room was broken into. I don't believe in coincidence."

Neither did she. "I had hoped to make another trip out to the land for photos. My uncle is breathing down my neck." He'd never been this obsessed with a land purchase before. Suspicion nagged at the edges of her mind.

"Although I've only been in Misty Hollow about a year, I've fallen in love with this place. Would you mind if I helped you dig through the notes?" Hope sparked in his eyes.

That would mean spending a lot of time with this handsome cowboy. Usually, Pressley preferred working alone. Despite her resolve, she nodded. "Can the ranch spare you?"

"I have vacation time coming."

She widened her eyes. "You'd spend your vacation researching the history of a mine where someone shot at you in order to keep you away?"

"Sure." He grinned. "Adds excitement."

She would never understand men. "Okay. We can start tomorrow. What makes you love this town so much?"

"My great-grandfather owned cotton fields once upon a time, then my grandfather changed to rice farming down in the bottom lands. My father moved to Texas for a bit. It wasn't until the Rocking W Ranch opened that I saw my opportunity to come here."

"What's your dream, River? Are you content to work for Mr. Wyatt forever?"

He frowned. "No, while I love horses, I'm not cut

out to be a rancher. I love tinkering with old cars, so I thought maybe I'd open my own business restoring vintage automobiles. What about you?"

"I've always wanted to be a photographer. That's why I want to go back out to the land. To take pictures that puts the place in its best possible light. A picture really is worth a thousand words, in my opinion." She polished off her breakfast and sat back. "I'll go with you to the sheriff, but please don't tell him I've made copies or kept the journal. I'll turn the journal in when we're finished."

"Okay, but I'm sure we're breaking a law or two." He tossed a tip on the table and slid from the booth. "Want to ride with me? I can drop you back off here when we're finished. Today is my day off. I'll let Wyatt know later that I'm taking my vacation. I have one or two things to finish up at the ranch, then I'm all yours."

Her heart skipped a beat. Heat rushed to her face. No man had ever said he was all hers. "I'll need my leather coverings before we head to the mine, and I also need to make a quick phone call. Meet you outside." She grabbed her things and rushed out the door.

Her uncle answered on the third ring. "What have you found out?"

"Proof that somebody doesn't want me snooping around that mine." She told him about River being shot at.

"Why was he even there? Don't get others involved, Pressley. This is our business."

"Children have been known to go out there, Uncle Frank. River was simply being cautious."

"Then have him board up the entrance to keep people out." Click.

~

"Why are you getting involved with that outsider?" Fred Murphy crossed his arms.

River waved a dismissive hand. "Give her a chance, Fred. She's wanting to learn this town's history, not destroy it."

The man didn't look convinced. "You trying to tell me she wants to preserve this town's history?"

"Sure." At least he did, and River was pretty sure he could convince Pressley to look at things in his way. "Wouldn't you like to know what really happened at the Duncan mine? Why folks die who spend time out there?"

"Yeah, but...she's not from around here."

"Neither am I."

"Yeah, but you've proven yourself by helping the sheriff when trouble comes calling. You're one of us now."

Nothing could make River happier. "I'll make sure she doesn't do any harm. Tell folks to lighten up, okay?"

"We're trusting you on this." Fred swiveled his barstool back to the counter and dug into his eggs and bacon.

River joined a pacing Pressley in the parking lot. "What's wrong?"

"My uncle wants me to ask you to board up the entrance to the mine and then stay away. He wants you to stay away, not me." She made a growling noise in her throat. "I hate to say this, but there's something going on that he isn't telling me."

"The land is worth a lot of money, especially if the mine hasn't been mined out. Could be he's overzealous."

"Maybe." She didn't look convinced. "He's headed overseas on business in a week. I may have to make a trip to the office." She tossed up her hands. "Or I'm looking for trouble where none exists."

River held his truck's passenger side door open. "I told someone you were going to focus on preserving the history of Misty Hollow."

"Why would you do that? Once the purchase is complete, I'll be headed back to Memphis."

"This way you won't incur so much opposition." He intended to preserve the history with or without her help, but it would be easier with help.

The sheriff's office was hopping, and he had to park on the street rather than in the parking lot. River considered coming back at another time, but being shot at was serious, and the sheriff needed to know. He shoved his door open.

Pressley climbed out before he could help her. "You talk to him alone. I'm a horrible liar, and if he asks about the papers, I'll spill everything."

River chuckled. "Okay. It shouldn't take long for me to file a report."

They entered the building together. Pressley found a spot near the vending machine to wait for him. River approached the receptionist and asked to see the sheriff.

"You and everyone else. Must be a full moon tonight because this town has gone crazy. Most of the complaints have to do with that lady you came in with. Folks think she's here to stir things up."

"They would be wrong." He spoke loudly so others could hear. "She's simply here to preserve history."

Grumbles rose behind him.

He turned to face those queued up at the reception desk. Maybe he should've had Pressley wait in the truck. "Look, folks. Miss Hamilton is simply here to help Misty Hollow, not burn the place to the ground." He pointed at his face. "Someone took a shot at me last night, and I want to know who. If it was one of you, then we have a bigger problem than whether or not this lady's company wants to buy the Duncan property."

"River, my office." The sheriff beckoned from the hallway. "Bring Miss Hamilton."

Pressley stared at the floor as she made herself as small as possible and followed the sheriff ahead of River. He tossed another stern look at those gathered in front of the reception desk. He'd meant what he'd said if he found out one of them was the shooter.

"What's this I hear about you getting shot at?" Sheriff Westbrook sat in his chair.

"Pressley and I were at the mine with the Wyatt twins and heard some screams and moans. Sounded a lot like a cougar's caterwauls but not natural." River lowered into a chair across from him. "I went back to investigate and found this." He set the speaker on the desk. "When I stepped from the mine, someone shot at me."

The sheriff's eyes flashed, then transferred to the speaker.

"My uncle has asked that I board up the mine," Pressley said.

"I'll have a deputy do that. With River being shot at, the place is now a crime scene."

She groaned. "My uncle will not like that at all."

"Tell him to feel free to call me, but I don't take

kindly to folks in my county getting shot at." He lifted his gaze. "I want both of you to stay away from there. The land isn't the property of Hamilton Enterprises yet, ma'am. When and if I'm convinced there's nothing fishy about the place, I'll reconsider."

"What about the property itself? I need to take pictures."

"As long as you stay away from the mine, I have no objection. Unless—" he speared her, then River with a warning glance. "It becomes dangerous. Then, the whole place will be denied to you. Got it?"

"Yes, sir." River stood. "Pressley and I are going to delve deep into the history of the place. We'll let you know if we find anything suspicious."

"Uh-huh. And how, exactly, do you plan to find that history? The last Duncan is dead."

"I've already spoken to Ms. Whatley." Pressley rose to her feet. "She was very helpful. I'm sure the library and the internet can tell me more."

Pressley might think she wasn't good at lying, but she was very good at skirting around the truth. River smiled. "I'll make sure she stays out of trouble."

"Do that."

He also had a strong feeling he might enjoy doing so. Spending time with Pressley might not be a bad vacation after all.

Chapter Seven

River knocked on Pressley's motel room at exactly seven the next morning. Not being a morning person in the slightest, she opened the door a few inches, mumbled something incoherent, and returned to the bathroom to finish getting ready.

"I thought we could take the photocopies and journal to the diner. We can sit at a back booth and have plenty of room to spread things out." His voice drifted from the front part of the room.

Pressley rolled her eyes and started to apply a small amount of makeup. She couldn't remember the last time she'd gone anywhere without lipstick.

"The diner gets busy, but as long as we buy something, even if it's coffee, Lucy won't run us off."

Pressley sighed and pulled her hair into a messy bun. When did the usually quiet River become so talkative? "You must be really excited about this history search." She stepped from the bathroom and slid the papers and journal into a large canvas bag.

"Aren't you? History is fascinating."

"This history could be dangerous."

He shrugged. "Could be, but that won't stop me. Not unless the danger gets too close to you."

"Don't let that stop you." Her room had already been broken into. If someone decided to shoot at her, Uncle Frank could send someone else to take her place in Misty Hollow.

"You're cranky in the mornings." He grinned and opened the door. After peering both ways, he stepped out and held it open for her.

"Once I have my first cup of coffee, I'm good." She glanced at his strong profile. "Wouldn't the library be a better place to do our research? We could use the computers."

"We'll get there." He grinned. "I have an ulterior motive for the diner."

"Would you mind sharing?" She arched a brow.

"Once the townspeople find out what we're doing, they're going to flock to our table to tell us what they know."

Smart. "What little digging I've done so far shows that mine had a dark history even before the legend of the doomed lovers."

"That's the fascination of the place." He opened the passenger side door to his truck so she could climb in. "I'm sure a lot of what we hear will be more of the same, but some of what the people tell us will be true."

"Hopefully, we can tell fact from fiction." Digging into the history didn't help with the purchase of the land, but it would fill her time until she received further orders from her uncle. It still nagged at her that he seemed more interested in the mine than the actual property, though. What was he not telling her?

A trip to Memphis was definitely something she

wanted to do when he flew overseas. There would be no better time to go through his files and see what he was really up to.

At the diner, they chose the booth the farthest from the door and settled in. River suggested they order breakfast before spreading out the papers. "The place should be full of old-timers by then."

She glanced around. "There are mostly old folks in here now."

"Just wait. You'd think they'd be here by now, but a lot of them wait until morning chores are done at the farm, then they congregate here." He perused at the menu. "The three eggs, bacon, hash browns, and toast, please."

"Chocolate gravy and biscuits." Pressley smiled at the waitress. "Best chocolate gravy around."

The server smiled. "I'll tell the chef you said so." When she brought their breakfasts, she said, "The chef said no charge this time."

"Thank you." Pressley took a deep breath of the warm chocolate and melted butter scent, then dug in.

When they'd finished, she pulled the papers from her bag and handed them to River. "The mine was dug in the late 1800s by a man named Colville. He lost the mine in a poker game to the first Duncan owner who made the mine profitable. When someone shot him, one of his kin retaliated, killing the shooter, and continued mining. It's this man who allegedly was one of the lovers. The woman was a young girl by the name of Ruby Lewis."

"That was my grandmother's sister." An elderly woman piped in, on her way back from the ladies room. "That whole story is hogwash. She never loved Roger

Duncan. Aunt Ruby loved Wilbur Wilson, one of the other miners. She went to see him when the mine caved in. Ten people died that day, not just Ruby and Duncan. Or so my family's stories go."

Pressley shot River an appreciative look. He'd nailed how folks in the diner would respond when they heard what they were doing. "Can you tell us anything else? We really want to get the information correct."

Her penciled-on brows rose to the edge of her dyed, inky hair—not shiny like River's but dull. The woman lowered her voice and leaned close. "Some say the mine was caved-in on purpose. Folks had heard rumblings and explosions during the days before."

"Not true," A man yelled from the booth next to him. "My grandfather was in charge of the explosives. He would not have let that happen. Those kind of accusations ruined his life."

"Well, I didn't start the rumors, Dick." The woman frowned. "So, mind your own business. I'm trying to talk."

Other voices joined in.

River stood. "We don't want to start a feud here, folks. We're here to listen to everyone, but one at a time, please."

The arguing escalated until Lucy stepped from the kitchen, put two fingers to her lips, and let out a shrill whistle. "Settle down now, or I'll run all y'all out of here. Take a number from the hostess and wait for River to call you." She shot Pressley and River an exasperated look, then returned to the kitchen.

Pressley dug in her purse for a pen and notepad. Things were going better than she could've hoped for.

~

He glared over the rim of his coffee cup. He hadn't spent all this time trying to keep folks away from the mine for this nosy woman to arrive in town and ruin everything. All he needed was proof the mine was still mineable and that he was the legal heir of the Duncan mine, and he'd be a very rich man. No one was going to take that away from him.

Once all these people started tossing out names, it was only a matter of time before the cowboy and the woman put the pieces together and came to ask him questions.

He finished his coffee and waved to the server for a refill. What he wanted to do was head up to the mine and resume his search, but staying here and listening to all the stories seemed more prudent. Not to mention the fact the sheriff's department was still looking around for evidence of who'd shot at the cowboy.

He shouldn't have aimed to miss!

With the cowboy gone, the woman wouldn't have the guts to continue. He needed to find a way to send her back to Memphis where she belonged. If he couldn't find a way, he'd make sure her body got lost in the mines never to be found again. Hers and that cowboy's.

~

Once order had been somewhat restored to the diner, things moved a lot smoother. There were still some dirty looks and a few words of dispute tossed around, but for the most part, folks came one by one to the table when River called their number.

So far, they'd learned the two "lovers" were nothing more than part of a legend. Several stories collaborated that fact. Also, there seemed to have been a feud between the Duncans and the Colvilles—a feud that had still existed until the late Roger Duncan's death.

"I think Colville killed Duncan." A man in faded coveralls pulled up a chair. "Who else would harbor a grudge against a man who stayed to himself? Those Duncans always were hermits."

"Have you told the sheriff your suspicions?" River glanced over to see Pressley writing.

"Do you think I should have?"

"Yes. Anything that could help their investigation should be brought to their attention."

"I'll go there just as soon as we're finished." He folded his hands on the table. "Here's a bit of news you probably haven't heard."

Pressley's eyes widened. Her pen stopped scratching across the paper.

"Some folks don't believe Roger Duncan was the last one. Some say his grandfather and his father before him both had illegitimate children. One of them had a son."

"Any idea who that could be?" River motioned for his coffee cup to be refilled.

"Nope. It's just a rumor, but my father used to say that all rumors were based on fact to some degree. You might want to do some digging in that direction. Oh, and a lot of folks around here call that mine The Devil's Entrance. Doorway to Hell is another cute nickname. Actually, it's most likely an extinct volcano crater, but superstition still runs strong in these mountains."

He pushed to his feet. "Look for someone with a brown spot in the white part of their eye. It's a family trait." He gave a nod, then ambled out of the diner.

"Think we're getting somewhere, River." Pressley's eyes sparkled. "We're going to solve the mystery of the Duncan mine."

"While you're doing that—" Lucy stopped at their table. "Why not do something really valuable and volunteer on the Fourth of July committee? I could use the help. Since you've chosen to use my diner as your meeting place, it's the least you can do. It would help raise your reputation in the eyes of these people, too, Pressley. As you can tell, they all love this town."

"What do you say?" River shrugged. "Want to help?"

"Suppose I can. I doubt my uncle will call me back to Memphis by then."

River smiled. "You have yourself two helpers, Lucy."

"Good." Her eyes lit up. "Possum pie on the house coming right up."

"I love possum pie." Pressley patted her stomach. "That rich chocolate…if I stay in Misty Hollow much longer, someone will have to roll me back to Memphis."

River tilted his head. "I doubt that. You could stand to gain a few pounds." Tall and willowy, she looked like a big wind would blow her away.

"You flatter me." Her cheeks turned pink as she returned to her notes. "I think we're done for the day. What's next? Did you have any trouble getting vacation time off?"

"Nope. Since I don't work with the summer camps or overnight camping trips unless someone else is out, they won't miss me too much. Not unless a vehicle breaks down. If it does, I'll work on it in the evenings. Digging up the town's history is a nice change of pace for me." He slid from the booth. "As for what's next…how about I show you some of the sights before taking you back to the motel?"

"Sure. I'd love that." She slid everything back into her bag and followed him outside.

Since he didn't want Pressley's entire time in Misty Hollow to be work, he drove to the lake, one of his favorite places. Despite it being the end of June, a breeze blew across the surface of the water, keeping it from being too warm.

A crane flew low, complaining about them disturbing its fishing. A few boats floated past the shore. Across the lake, a person could just make out the campground filled with tents and campers.

Pressley approached the bank. "This is a beautiful place."

"There's a homeless camp past the campground. The sheriff doesn't run them off as long as they don't cause trouble."

"Everyone needs a place to live," she said, brushing a strand of hair out of her face. "Even if it's a cardboard box. If it's something they can call their own, it means something."

"You sound as if you have experience."

"No. I just haven't had the opportunity to settle down. My job keeps me on the move. Motels and hotels have been my home for the last couple of years."

He didn't know why he took her hand in his, but it felt right for the two of them to stand there watching the water, and just be.

Chapter Eight

Pressley hadn't realized how lonely she'd been until she'd spent time at the lake with River the day before. She hadn't minded her solitary life of living from a suitcase. It allowed her to see the country. But, standing by the lake, her hand tucked in his, had opened her eyes to the possibility of something better.

Could she leave the big-city life behind and move to a small town of around twenty-five thousand people? She laughed, jumping ahead of herself. No doubt River had been caught up in the beauty and romance of the lake same as she. Who knew if he wanted anything more than someone who shared his love of digging up history and solving mysteries?

Besides, they'd known each other less than a month. No one formed a romantic relationship in that time outside of romance novels.

She peered out the window. River should be arriving at any minute to pick her up for breakfast before driving her to the land. Mine or not, she still had a job to do and hadn't made a dent in photographing the acreage.

Eventually, Uncle Frank would be able to sign the final papers, and Pressley needed to have the information he requested. River's truck pulled into view, and she stepped from her room, locking the door behind her.

"Good morning." She hurried down the stairs, climbed into her seat, and clicked her seatbelt into place.

He eyed the leather chaps in her lap. "Good morning. I see you're ready."

"Yep." She grinned. "I'm excited, actually. This job is taking longer than any other I've done."

"Have you considered calling Duncan's lawyer? He might have an idea when things can wrap up." He turned the truck around and headed for the diner.

"I have not. That's a great idea." When he parked in front of the diner, she headed for the nearby picnic tables. "Let's eat outside this morning. I can call the lawyer while we wait for our food without anyone listening in on the conversation."

"Do you want the biscuits and gravy again?"

"No, whatever the special is, thanks." She pulled her phone from her purse and dialed the number for Mr. Duncan's lawyer.

"Stern and Associates," a perky voice answered.

"Mr. Stern, please. Tell him Pressley from Hamilton Enterprises is calling."

"Hold, please." Soft elevator music played.

River had returned before Mr. Stern answered and sat across from Pressley, placing a cup of coffee in front of her. "Server will be here shortly."

She nodded absently. "Thank you for taking my call, Mr. Stern. I'm calling to see where we're at in the proceedings following Mr. Duncan's untimely death."

"It's moving along."

"Someone else is handling his affairs? A family member? I wasn't aware there were any."

"I cannot say anything more than that someone has come forward claiming a right to the acreage. Until his claim is proven one way or the other, we cannot proceed. However, I don't see it taking much longer."

Pressley frowned. "To clarify…someone is claiming to be part of the Duncan family?"

"Yes, but I can't divulge their identity. Since they have now hired us to represent them, it would be a violation of attorney-client privilege."

"A person has come forth making a claim to the land, and you are now representing them as well as Mr. Duncan's affairs? Isn't that a conflict of interest?"

"I know it sounds complicated, Miss Hamilton, but if this person is indeed a relative, there isn't as much conflict as you would think." Impatience laced his words. "I have a full schedule, Miss Hamilton. Is there anything else?"

"Am I permitted to continue photographing the land in preparation for the sale to go through?" The last thing she needed was to be arrested for trespassing.

"Unless the owner states otherwise, then yes. Since we don't have a legitimate owner at this time, there shouldn't be a problem. I'll notify your company if you need to cease. Have a good day." He hung up.

"Well?" River asked.

"Someone has come forward laying claim to the land." She stirred sugar and cream into her coffee. "I guess the rumors about an illegitimate heir must be true."

"Unless they don't want us to know who they are—"

"Or we see a brown dot in their eye..." Which seemed far-fetched to her. She sighed. "At least for now, I'm still able to proceed on my end." Uncle Frank would not be pleased. "Excuse me while I make another call." She got up from the table and moved a few feet away.

Her uncle had already received the news and was not pleased. "Get the job done before we're ordered away."

"When did you find out?"

"Last night. I would've called you later today. Will you be able to complete the job?"

"The photographs? Yes. I'm headed up there this morning."

"I'm talking about the mine."

"The sheriff has ordered us to stay away."

"Then don't get caught." Click.

She frowned at the silent phone in her hand. Her uncle had just demanded that she break the law. "This whole thing grows more unbelievable by the minute." She filled River in as she took her seat, then stopped talking when the server arrived with their breakfast. When the server left, she continued. "My uncle told me to return to the mine to take pictures."

"What if there's crime-scene tape across the entrance?"

"He doesn't seem to care. I'm not crazy about getting on the wrong side of the sheriff." She stared at the ham and cheese omelet in front of her, appetite gone.

"Neither am I." He crossed his arms. "Maybe

he'll be content with photos of the outside."

"Hopefully, because at this point, that's all he's going to get."

~

The more River heard about this uncle of Pressley's, the less he liked the man. There seemed to be something shady about the whole mine dealings. If the man was on the up and up, why not wait until all the details were worked out? If they didn't go his way, why not find other land? Because it all had to do with the mine. His mind flicked to the chunk of quartz he'd found. If there were more, enough to reopen the mine, then that would explain a lot. He shoved open his truck door wanting very much to enter the mine, but like Pressley, he didn't want to get on the sheriff's bad side.

"What's wrong?" Pressley pulled her chaps on over the leggings she wore.

"I'm uncertain as to how to proceed."

"In what way?"

"I really want to go deeper into that mine." He exhaled slowly and closed the door to his truck. "I have a feeling this isn't about the land at all, but about the quartz."

"You're thinking the mine can be opened again?" She slung her camera strap around her neck and shouldered her bag.

"Yep." He met her gaze. "If I'm right, things are going to get ugly. The prospect of a lot of money tends to bring out the worst in people." He prayed he was wrong and the quartz he'd discovered was all there was to be found.

"That would explain my uncle's insistence I enter the mine. He wants proof there's money to be made other than building houses." Her eyes widened. "I feel like quitting."

"Not until we find out what's really going on here. Ready?" He put a booted foot on the barbed-wire fence, pressing down and pulling up the top wire for her to crawl through.

"He's going to get a piece of my mind when I call him next." Pressley bent and eased her way through the wire. "I'm going to demand he be straight with me." She turned and held the wires apart for River.

"Lead the way. I'll follow you at your pace."

She smiled over her shoulder. "I'm headed for the mine. I'll take photos along the way, but this whole business is centered around that mine. What's the worst that could happen? The sheriff yells at us?"

"He could arrest us."

"Scared?" She arched a brow.

"Nope." He laughed, enjoying her spirit. "But, I don't want to be fired."

"I'm only teasing. We won't go inside." She headed through the tall grass ahead of him.

A few yards in, she screamed and jumped back. "Snake! Get back."

He pulled the handgun from the holster he wore on his hip and fired.

"That—" She pointed with a trembling hand. "That is why I wear these leathers. I could've died."

"You wouldn't have died unless you were allergic to that kind of snake. Most people don't die from a copperhead bite." His heart raced at the thought of her being bitten. Snakes were a part of living in Arkansas, and he rarely gave them a second thought. "You okay?"

"Yes." She eyed the dead serpent and gave it a

wide berth. "Did you have to shoot it, though? We're in its territory."

He froze. Did he hear her correctly? Here he was being gallant, and she was worried about him killing the snake. "Sorry?"

"I'm being silly, I know." She stopped and snapped a few photos. "Do you think anyone heard the gun go off?"

"If they're close enough, but gunshots aren't exactly a rare thing out here. Lots of folks target practice." He moved ahead of her in order to keep a look out for more snakes. "If you keep talking, you'll scare away anything that might harm you."

"Except for people."

"True." Although, he didn't expect to see anyone.

"What's that?" Pressley pointed to the entrance of the mine where yellow crime-scene tape fluttered in the breeze. "A sign? Would the sheriff's department have put up a sign?"

"Stay here." River marched toward what definitely looked like a hand-painted sign.

Pressley followed. "*Warning. Do Not Enter. Trespassers will be shot.*" She clutched River's arm. "Can they do that? As of right now, this mine doesn't have an owner. Can they threaten to shoot?"

"Looks like they can." He turned in a slow circle, studying the ground around them.

It hadn't rained in days, making finding footprints impossible. A few broken twigs showed someone or something had recently passed, but he found nothing more to help him figure out who could've left the sign. "We'll have to alert the sheriff."

Pressly's shoulders slumped. "That's it then. He'll

definitely make sure we don't come this way again." She pulled up her camera and stepped closer to the entrance. The flash from her camera lit up the inside.

"Keep doing that. Let me see what I can." Plus, they'd have the photos to study. He put a hand against the mine entrance and stared inside as she snapped photo after photo. "Point the camera toward the ground." Sure enough, the flash lit up a set of footprints in the damp ground inside the mine. Someone had been there within the last day or two. Someone who had disregarded the yellow crime-scene tape strung across the entrance. The back of his neck prickled. "I think we have enough. Let's get out of here."

"Are you sure? If I take a couple of steps in, I might be able to get some better photos of the tunnel. You could be the lookout."

"My gut tells me it's time to go." He grabbed her by the arm and pulled her away.

"Okay." She replaced the lens cover on her camera.

A shot rang out, kicking up dust at her feet.

Her eyes widened and her mouth fell open.

River dove, tackling her to the ground. "Don't move."

"Believe me, I won't." She squirmed out from under him and aimed her camera in the direction the shot had come from. "This camera has a great telephoto lens. Especially in the daylight." She snapped a few photos.

"Don't you ever listen? I told you not to move."

"I thought you meant for me to stay down." She took a few more pictures, before replacing the cap. "Let's get these developed."

The woman's stubbornness would be the death of him.

Chapter Nine

Pressley peered through the peephole in the door when someone knocked. Seeing River, she opened the door. "You need to see these photos. I walked over and had them developed last night—"

"Alone?" He frowned.

"Yes. It was still daylight. I was fine. You have to see this." She grabbed his hand and dragged him to the table. "What do you see?"

"Bad guys do go out in daylight, Pressley." He peered at the photos, then with narrowed eyes, leaned closer. "You got the shooter?"

"Sort of. He's too far away to get details, but I'm sure the sheriff will want to see these. Did you call him yet?"

"No. I thought we'd go together, but it turns out, there's a council meeting this morning regarding some issues in town, and he'll be there." He lifted a photo for a closer look. "You have some good ones of the tunnel into the mine."

"I wish we could've gone inside. You can't see too much, other than the fact that someone has been in there." She grinned. "Footprints. Fuzzy, but I'm sure that's what they are." She tilted her head. "What kind of issues?'

His brow furrowed. "Seems like there's more activity at the mine than we thought. The Wyatt twins were out there after we left and were scared off by gunfire."

"Who would shoot at kids?" Her mouth dropped open. "That's horrible."

"Yep. Word is Sheriff Westbrook wants some heads to roll, hence the town meeting." His mouth quirked. "Think he might be blaming us for digging up all the history and speculation."

"There is no way that this is our fault." She refused to believe so. "I'm simply doing my job—one he's well aware of. We didn't disobey him by entering the mine, so he has no reason to be angry with us. He needs to focus on the person behind this."

"Settle down, Rambo." He chuckled. "I'm only passing on what I've heard."

"Hmph." She gathered up the photos and put them in her bag. Having made duplicates, these copies were for the sheriff. She still couldn't believe someone would shoot at a couple of children. Their father must be fit to be tied. "I'm ready."

"Since the meeting is early, I have doughnuts and coffee in the truck." River held the door open for her.

"A man after my own heart." She stiffened. What was wrong with her? This was not the time for flirtation, mild or otherwise. Pressley gave herself a mental shake. She'd been spending so much time with River she'd become used to him. *Comfortable.* That wouldn't do. No emotional attachments. She didn't plan on staying in Misty Hollow once her assignment was finished.

The town meeting was held in the high school multi-purpose room. Almost every slot of the parking lot held a vehicle, even a tractor and a couple of recreational vehicles.

Pressley climbed from the truck without waiting for River's assistance. They were working together, nothing more. A working partner wouldn't open the door for her. Well, River would. She stifled a sigh and followed him into the building.

Sheriff Westbrook stood off to one side eyeing everyone who entered. Spotting them, he strode their way, his hat clutched in his hand. "I'd like a word with you."

"We'd like to talk to you, too." She dug in her bag for the photos. "I took these at the mine yesterday. No, we did not step one foot inside. I was simply doing my job and managed to snap a photo of the shooter. Yes, he shot at us…again." She lowered her voice as several people passing by slowed.

"Can we identify him?" He flipped through the pictures.

"I don't think so. Not unless you know him. He's kind of far away. You can also tell someone has been nosing around inside the mine despite the crime-scene tape."

"Like the Wyatt twins."

She tapped one of the photos. "Man-size prints. I'm getting close to finding out who wants to keep people away from that mine, Sheriff. Once I do, we'll know why."

"You, Miss Hamilton, will not investigate this."

His eyes flashed. "River, I'm holding you to the task of making sure she doesn't. Unless you have the same foolish intent, which could get you both killed." He met River's gaze as if expecting him to agree to babysit Pressley.

"I do not need someone to watch me, sir." She squared her shoulders. "I think I have enough photos of the land; if not, I'll go back up there. Rest assured, I will not enter the mine until it is the property of Hamilton Enterprises."

"Nor will you enter if it's a crime scene." High spots of color appeared on his cheeks. "I will arrest you, ma'am."

"Duly noted."

~

He had to get those photographs. That idiot woman. Did he have to shoot someone in order to get people to back off?

And those kids! Why didn't their father make them stay away? Accidents happened in mines all the time—whatever it took to take back what rightfully belonged to him. He found a seat between two overweight women in the second row and squeezed in. "Excuse me."

The women frowned and clutched their purses close to their laps but gave him a bit of room. The cloying scent of their perfume threatened to choke him. He cleared his throat, dug a handkerchief from the pocket of his coveralls, and pretended he had the sniffles in order to cover his nose.

The rancher Wyatt and his family sat in the front row in reserved seats like royalty. Ha. The land his ranch sat on had also once belonged to the Duncan family, but it had been sold a long time ago, not stolen.

The conversations and murmurs died down as the sheriff took his spot behind the podium on the stage. "Folks, I'll make this meeting as short as possible, but there are some important issues that need to be addressed, and it will take this town working together to solve the problem."

Let them try to ferret him out. He smiled behind his handkerchief.

~

River escorted Pressley to a seat in the fifth row as Sheriff Westbrook took his place at the front of the room.

"I can't believe he told you to watch over me." Pressley scoffed, "As if I were a child in need of a sitter."

"We're more like partners in crime, don't you think?' He grinned, then sobered. "It is getting dangerous, though. If that guy will shoot at a couple of kids—" He shook his head. "I agree with the sheriff— It's time for us to stay away from that land and mine. At least for a while."

"That's fine. I want to take a trip to Memphis while my uncle is gone. He's hiding something, and I intend to find out what. There shouldn't be any shooting involved." She stared at the sheriff who tapped the microphone before starting to speak.

"Can everyone hear me?"

Heads nodded.

"Good. I'll get right to the point. No one, I repeat no one—" his gaze flicked from the Wyatt twins to River and Pressley—"Are to be anywhere near the Duncan mine. In fact, stay away from that land altogether. You will be trespassing. People are being shot at. Yesterday, someone took a shot at not only River and Miss Hamilton, but also at the Wyatt boys. This is unacceptable."

Shouts of outrage filled the room.

The sheriff raised a hand for silence. "If anyone knows something that might help us catch the person responsible, please contact the sheriff's office."

"Do we have trouble in our town again?" A man in faded jeans and a flannel shirt stood. "Because it seems like it's become the norm here. It's your job to keep this town safe. That's what we elected you for."

"Horace, sit down. I know my job. Together this town can handle one man who seems to believe the mine belongs to him, don't you think? I'm not saying I want anyone acting like a vigilante. Just keep your eyes and ears open. Can we do that?"

Heads nodded.

"Good. Now, Lucy will come up here and talk a bit about the upcoming Fourth of July celebration before everyone continues on with their day." He stepped from the podium and went to stand near the door.

Lucy took his place, her scarlet hair shining bright under the lights. "We do this every year, so things should run smoothly. River Swanson and Pressley Hamilton are in charge this year and will be needing volunteers. There's a signup sheet on a table in the back of the room. Take a look and sign up for something. The success of this celebration depends on you. The diner will again cater sandwiches and finger foods."

River glanced at Pressley. "I don't recall saying we wanted to be in charge."

"Me neither. Thought we were only helping. I have no idea what goes on at small town celebrations. You'll have to take the lead."

"I don't know." Good grief. Maybe Mrs. White could help. The thought of being in charge and failing scared him more than someone shooting at him.

"This is going to take time away from our investigating. Not to mention my uncle will have a coronary when he finds out my whole focus isn't on the mine."

He patted her hand. "It'll be fine. I'll find us help." Lots of it. "The other ranch hands will help if I ask." He hoped, although he suspected this sort of thing was out of all their comfort zones.

"We could always let it leak that we know…things. Stuff about the mine. People will volunteer to help out of sheer nosiness." A pert smile spread across her face. "Plus, it might draw out the shooter so we can catch him."

"You're a dangerous woman, Pressley Hamilton."

"Scared?" She arched a brow as she stood.

"No." Absolutely, but his fear had more to do with his growing feelings for her than the danger of trying to find the identity of the man shooting at anyone who got close to the mine.

They headed for the signup sheet and stood behind the table. Soon, a line formed.

"We're planning on doing something historical for this year's celebration," Pressley said. "Something that highlights why we love this town, the rumors surrounding the mine…maybe a reenactment of the doomed lovers…so sign up to be included." She smiled at everyone who passed.

Several stopped and formed a line.

River chuckled. She really did have a devious mind. His smile faded. She wouldn't expect him to act in her little show, would she? His blood drained to his feet. No way would he take part in that. He'd put his foot down. She could find someone who'd grown up in Misty Hollow. Someone who had more of a stake in the town's history than he did. No way would she get him on a stage of any kind.

"What's wrong?" She peered up at him, concern in her eyes. "The color has drained from your face. Are you ill?"

"Nope."

"Are you sure?" She put the back of her hand against his cheek. "You look so pale."

"I'm fine." He pulled her hand down. "It's just warm in here."

"Okay. We're finished." The line had dissipated. "We've quite a few signatures. All we have to do now is set up a meeting time to go over things. I'm sure Lucy will let us meet at the diner. It's good business for her."

"Yeah." His breathing returned to normal. He had nothing to worry about. There were plenty of signatures on that paper.

Chapter Ten

Pressley waited at the window for River, then opened the door as he strode toward the door. "I appreciate you driving me, but it's going to be a very long day. At least five hours to get there. You won't be home until really late."

"Don't worry about me. I've stayed up twenty-four hours before." He grinned and took her bag to stow in the backseat of his truck. "If we have to, we can spend the night in Memphis. Do some sightseeing."

"I've seen everything in Memphis, thank you." All she wanted to do was prove her uncle wasn't being forthright with her, return to Misty Hollow for her things, and get back to a semblance of a normal life. Or did she? Pressley cut River a sideways glance as she climbed into the front passenger seat. She'd gotten used to and enjoyed his company every day.

"I haven't seen the sights." He removed his cowboy hat and set it on the console between them. "Working on the ranch keeps me busy most of the time."

"Until I came along. Your vacation time should be

almost over, right?"

"Yeah." He sighed and backed from the motel. "Don't worry. I'll still help with the Fourth of July celebration."

"You bet you will. After all, you got us into that whole thing." She smiled, not really minding. It had been a long time since she'd had time to celebrate much of anything except a new land purchase for Hamilton Enterprises.

"It'll be fun." He pointed at a bag at her feet. "Breakfast burritos from the diner. And coffee. Can't forget the coffee."

"You are truly a prince." No man had ever thought of her comfort the way he did. Maybe she shouldn't be in such a hurry to leave Misty Hollow. The men here were certainly of a different breed than she was used to. She unwrapped the burritos and handed him one. "Coffee?"

"Already in the thermos. Thanks." He took the food in his left hand.

In a little under five hours, they pulled up in front of the building complex that was Hamilton Enterprises. The cement and glass structure llooked more suited for New York than the south, but Uncle Frank was big on appearances.

"Wow." River peered through the truck's windshield. "He must do well for himself."

"He does." She shoved her door open, then grabbed her bag from the backseat. "Let's do this. He should be in the air by now, leaving us plenty of time to snoop."

"What if we're caught?" He followed her to the building.

"Everyone here knows me. They won't think anything about us being there. The offices are on the fourth floor."

He paused at the elevator. "Are there stairs?"

"Afraid of elevators?"

"Closed spaces and lack of control, so yes."

"Okay." She wouldn't put pressure on him to ride in something that would make him uncomfortable. "The stairs are this way."

By the time they reached the fourth floor, her thighs burned, and her breathing came in gasps. River hardly seemed to be breathing hard at all.

She shot him a glare and leaned against the wall. "Give me a minute."

"Want me to carry you?" His mouth twitched.

"Don't you dare." She pushed away from the wall and forced herself to walk toward her uncle's office. This would be the last time she showed weakness. Being laughed at was at the top of things she hated.

"I was only teasing you." His voice still hint a trace of laughter.

"Well, stop it." She fished for the keys in her bag and unlocked the door to Hamilton Enterprises. "I don't like being teased."

"Oh, you shouldn't have told me that. Now, I'll want to tease you more." He chuckled.

"Stop it."

He laughed harder, drawing the attention of a woman in a suit who passed by them. "I feel out of place in my jeans and boots."

She couldn't imagine him wearing a suit, but if he did, she'd bet money he'd look stellar. "Come on." Pressley opened the door and stepped onto plush carpet that muffled their footsteps and led River past windowed offices to her uncle's at the end of a long hall. Since he planned on being gone for a few days, no one else was working. She and River had the place all to themselves. After unlocking the door to Uncle Frank's office, she moved to the other side of his walnut desk and stared at the locked drawer. If he had anything to hide, it would be in there.

"Where do you want me to look?" River stood in the center of the office and glanced around.

"The bookcases. We're looking for anything he might have on the Duncan mine—why he has a fascination about it. I think he wants the mine more than the land." She pulled a paper clip from a holder on the desk and straightened it. She'd watched some videos on how to pick a lock and hoped she could do it.

River riffled through books. "It would be cool if one of these opened a secret passage."

"It would, but don't get your hopes up. Uncle Frank isn't that imaginative." The lock on the drawer clicked. "Got it." She slid the drawer open as the sound of a toilet flushing came from the other side of the wall.

She froze.

Uncle Frank stepped from the bathroom, drying his hands on a paper towel. He scowled at River, then at her. "What are you doing?"

"I thought you were out of town." She stood and closed the drawer with her leg, hoping he wouldn't know what she was doing.

"I caught a later flight." He narrowed his eyes. "Are you snooping?" He stormed to her side.

They were caught. She might as well confess. "I want to know what your fascination is with the Duncan mine. So, yes, I'm here to snoop."

He raised his hand and slapped her across the face. "You're fired!"

She put a hand to her cheek. Tears blurred her vision. "I quit."

~

River took two steps and laid a quick right fist to the side of Frank Hamilton's jaw. "Do not touch her again. Hear me?"

The man's eyes flashed. "Get out of my office before I call the police."

"Are you going to answer my question?" Pressley lifted her chin.

"Because of the riches, you stupid woman. The only reason I keep you around is because you can ferret out anything. But now that I know I can't trust you, we're done. Clean out your desk."

A slow smile spread across her face. "That means all the notes I've gathered. Oh, and the photographs. All which are my property now that I no longer work for you." She grabbed her bag from the chair she'd dropped it in. "Come on, River. This day won't be as long as previously thought."

"You'll regret this, Pressley. I guarantee it."

River put a hand on her back and glared at her uncle. "I meant what I said. Touch her again, and you'll answer to me." He'd strangle the man.

Pressley was right, though. Her uncle hadn't wanted the land. The mine was what he sought. Well, good luck. With Duncan's death, it could take weeks or months before he could get his hands on the property.

"You're more closely tied to this than you know," her uncle called after them.

"What do you mean?" Pressley swiveled to face him.

The man smiled. "Do some searching in the family tree, dear niece. Dig deep. You'll find we're descendants of the Colvilles." He pulled a file from a drawer and tossed it at their feet. "That land and mine belong to the Hamiltons."

Face pale, Pressley picked up the folder. "Let's go, River." She straightened and marched from the office.

"We can take the elevator." He was afraid she'd fall over if they took the stairs. "I can handle it for a few minutes."

"I'll be fine. The stairs are good." She headed in that direction.

He gripped her arm to stop her. "I insist, sweetheart." He pressed the button on the elevator. When the doors opened with a whoosh, he took a deep breath and ushered her inside. He plastered himself against the far wall and squeezed his eyes shut, leaving her to push the button.

"Hold the elevator!" A man in an ill-fitting suit rushed onto the elevator.

"Lobby?"

"Yes." His chest heaved.

River cracked his eyes open at the urgency in the man's voice.

As the elevator doors closed, he heard the sound of shouts and pounding feet. Someone screamed, "He's been shot!"

The man in the elevator with them pressed the button Pressley had several times as if by doing so he could speed up the elevator's descent.

Pressley frowned and moved to River's side. "Something's happened. What if it's Uncle Frank?"

The man with them whirled to face them. The beard he wore slid to the side. A disguise. His eyes hardened.

River's eyes narrowed.

The elevator doors opened.

The man backed out, then ran.

River put out an arm to stop Pressley as she started to step out. "Not yet. Something isn't right. Is there another way out?"

"There's a service elevator on the second floor that leads to stairs."

"We'll take that." He pressed the button to close the doors.

"But, you hate—"

"I'll be all right." He forgot his dislike of elevators over the strong feeling of danger. Something had happened on the fourth floor—something he and Pressley narrowly missed being a part of. The elevator stopped at the second floor. When the doors opened, River peered out. Seeing no one around, he took Pressley's hand and led her to a door with a sign that said stairs. The stairs led to the street. Again, he checked for anyone who might want to harm them, then led her at a jog to his truck. Sirens wailed in the distance. Once they were both safely inside, he squealed tires out of the parking lot, not relaxing until they reached the interstate. "You okay?" He cut her a glance.

"Yes." She opened the file.

A while later, she closed it. "Uncle Frank was right. My great grandfather was a Colville. His daughter married a Hamilton. But that land isn't ours. It was lost in a poker game. How can some people be so delusional?"

"Greed."

"Uncle Frank doesn't need the money."

"That isn't usually what matters. It's prestige, power." He reached over and gave her hand a squeeze. "How do you feel about losing your job?"

"I'm fine. He's fired me before. Once he realizes how much he needs me, he calls me back."

"Maybe you should call him. Tell him you read the file." He took the next exit off the interstate." You could call while I fill the tank with gas."

"I'll do that. Give him a chance to apologize." Her hand flew to her face. "He's never hit me before, though. That was a bit of a shock."

Rage filled him again. "He'd better not do it again."

"I don't think he knew what hit him when you threw that punch." She chuckled. "My uncle isn't used to being stood up to."

"No one mistreats a woman when I'm around." Especially one he cared for. He hadn't given a second thought to his actions. River had simply reacted on instinct. He pulled into a truck stop then stood next to his truck as he pumped gas. When he climbed back into the cab, Pressley faced him with wide eyes.

"Someone shot and killed my uncle. That's what happened while we were in the elevator. What if the man who got on with us is the killer?"

River would bet his boots that the man was, indeed, the killer. "The man in the elevator had a brown spot in the white of his right eye."

Chapter Eleven

Two days later, still in shock over her uncle's murder and having been grilled extensively by the Memphis Police Department, Pressley had been allowed to return to Misty Hollow. She and River had ridden the elevator with a murderer. Most likely the same man who'd shot at anyone getting close to the mine.

All proceedings on the purchase of the mine had halted. Lawyers had gotten involved trying to dig into the truth of who actually owned the land—something that could take months…years.

Pressley didn't want it. The place was tainted with centuries-old blood. She no longer wanted to be a part of Misty Hollow's Fourth of July celebration. If she hadn't been ordered to stay close for further questioning, she'd have packed up and moved home.

But, River was coming to pick her up for a celebration meeting—one focused on the re-enactment of the doomed lovers of old.

She tossed aside her sheet, all excitement gone. How could Uncle Frank be dead? Her eyes burned. The man might have been selfish, greedy, and crass, but he'd been the only family she'd had left. Except for the man with a brown spot in her eye who very well might be a distant cousin.

After a quick shower that did nothing to wash away the gloom left behind from her uncle's murder, she made coffee in the supplied coffeepot and sat by the window to wait. Cars rolled past on the road, their tires splashing in puddles left behind from the previous night's rain.

Pressley could've liked living in Misty Hollow. Before death tainted things. The only good thing about the place pulled up in a battered navy-blue truck. She set down the cup and gathered her things in her bag before greeting River.

"You okay?" He jumped out and rushed to open the passenger door for her. "It's been a rough few days."

"I'll be fine. It doesn't seem real yet." She climbed in, putting her bag on the floor at her feet. "It's nice of Lucy to let us have a breakfast meeting at the diner."

"It's good business for her." He studied her for a second, then closed the door.

The man usually knew when she didn't want to talk and respected her enough to let her be. Yes, River was the best part of this mountain town. Was she ready to give up their friendship? She studied him from lowered lashes. No, not really. The man wasn't only drop-dead gorgeous on the outside with that inky black hair and piercing blue eyes, but he was also beautiful on the inside. A real man not afraid to mention his fears, like his fear of elevators. She'd miss him when she left.

"It'll be okay." He gave her a sad smile and pulled away from the motel.

She nodded and stared out the window as the rain started again. At least she wouldn't be traipsing across the Duncan land in the wet. It was no use. A dark cloud of doom that had nothing to do with the weather refused to dissipate.

They entered the diner to stares. No smiles. Tension hung heavy in the air.

"What's wrong?" Pressley whispered.

"I don't know." River put a hand on the small of her back and guided her to a table near the door. "I'm sure we'll find out."

Did she want to? The looks on the people's faces reminded her of when she'd first arrived in town. "I think you should take the lead today."

When Lucy approached their table to take their order, the friendliness usually associated with her had also disappeared. "The special?"

"Okay." Pressley frowned. "Mind telling me what's going on?"

She stared without speaking for several long seconds. "You can answer that better than anyone, Miss Hamilton."

"Since I seem to be in the dark, maybe you could clarify." Pressley folded her hands on the table to stop their trembling.

"Word is that you're kin to the Colvilles. That makes it appear as if you're here simply to take back what you think belongs to you." She hitched her chin, causing her bright red hair to shimmy.

"I had no idea until my uncle told me minutes before someone murdered him. That's right.

Murdered." She drew out the last word, but she made sure she spoke loud enough for everyone in the diner to hear. "Did the gossip mill leave that part out?"

Lucy paled. "Apparently so."

"The killer rode in the elevator with us," River said. "We could have suffered the same fate as Mr. Hamilton. Pressley is the victim here, folks, not the one responsible for the shootings."

"The subject is closed." Sheriff Westbrook spoke up from the booth behind them. "Too much information makes our investigation difficult." He stood. "Miss Hamilton has nothing to do with the shootings. End of subject, and I'll hear no more about it. Most of you are here for a meeting. Get on with it." He sat back down, asking Lucy for a coffee refill.

The diner remained silent for a minute or so, then conversations resumed as if nothing had transpired. Pressley shook her head and whispered, "People are strange creatures."

"Still want me to take the lead this morning?"

"Yes." Pressley still didn't feel convinced she had these people's trust. No matter how she looked at things, she was the outsider here, even if she was related somehow to one of the town's founding fathers.

~

He'd been so close. She'd been within his reach, and he'd fled like a frightened buck. One pull of the trigger, and the last obstacle standing in his way could have been eliminated.

Hamilton had shouted that they were kin right before his life ended. Was he telling the truth? Did the woman have as much right to the land as he did?

It didn't matter. Soon, he'd be the only one left to

claim the deed. All he had to do was get rid of her without suspicion falling on him. He could act as surprised as anyone when he "accidentally" stumbled across the information naming him a relative of the original owner. Since no Duncans lived, it shouldn't be a problem, right? Worst case scenario—he had to purchase the land and hope because of all the trouble that no one else would make a bid.

So many things to consider. So many things that could go wrong.

He paced his living room, occasionally tossing glances out the window, certain someone out there knew his secret. That he'd made a mistake in Hamilton's office that would lead the authorities to his door. But if he ran, people would notice. If he didn't eat his meals at the diner, someone would come checking on him. He needed an excuse to order out. A plan to lay low until he could act on the final phase.

He snatched his birth certificate from the kitchen table. Imagine his surprise when he'd discovered it in his dead mother's Bible listing Davis Duncan, unrecognized son of Roger Duncan, as his father. It had felt good to kill the old man who'd rejected his birth father.

The mine belonged to him! To Roy Hyatt, son of Sylvia Hyatt, the poor girl from the wrong side of the tracks. It didn't matter. He'd made a name for himself. The people of Misty Hollow always called on Roy when they needed yard work or an odd job done. No one would suspect him of killing anyone.

That cowboy had gotten a good look at him. He'd have to be taken care of, same as the woman.

Misty Hollow loved Roy. Once he'd taken care of

the obstacles, he'd be rich. Maybe he'd do something marvelous for the town as penance.

~

"Sure, we'll help." Mrs. White glanced at Marilyn. "You'll need streamers and paper flowers. We'll get the women at church busy on that right away. I know someone who has a fireworks business." She patted River's shoulder. "You leave this up to us and focus on building a stage for the play you two want to put on. Why don't the two of you play the ill-fated lovers?" She wiggled her eyebrows.

"People have already signed up for that." Pressley's cheeks heated up. "River and I are writing the script, trying to keep it as accurate as possible."

"Speaking of—" Mrs. White reached into her apron pocket and pulled out folded sheets of paper. "Found some info at the library. Myrtle, the librarian, is as old as dirt and knew right where to find this." She handed it to Pressley.

"Thank you."

Mrs. White sobered. "You two be careful. Dark things happened at that mine. Blood was spilled. Anything that came out of there was tainted with evil."

River shuddered. "We'll take care." He had no intention of going back to the mine since there was no reason to. "Want to come out to the garage with me? I need to change the oil on the tractor. We can talk while I work."

"Okay." Pressley followed him, pausing at the corral to pet the horses.

"Do you ride?"

"Not since I was a teenager, and not very well or often, but I love horses."

He leaned on the railing. "What will you do now that your uncle is gone?"

She sighed and turned to face him. "Finish with the celebration, then head back to Memphis, I guess. Since I'm his only heir, a lawyer should contact me about his affairs."

"You should be left well off."

"Hmm. I'd rather have my bossy, unreasonable, selfish uncle." Tears sprang to her eyes, and she returned her attention to the horses. "Money is nice, but it's never been my focus. A job well done is what's important. To answer your question, I have no idea what I'll do when I return to Memphis. Find a new job, I suppose."

"Let's take a look at the papers Mrs. White gave you." Anything to take her mind off her troubles.

"Oh, wow." She turned the page so he could see. "This actually mentions the fight between the Colvilles and the Duncans. The reporter interviewed everyone involved, even the families of the dead couple." She raised wide eyes. "Here's a mention of my relative. My grandfather was his son."

River shrugged. "That reinforces what your uncle told you, but it also says the mine changed ownership with a bad hand of poker."

She nodded. "And my great-grandfather vowed revenge. Do you think he caused the cave-in that killed those lovers?"

"Remember, the gal loved another man. I don't think she was meant to be a victim." Tragic, really. Poor woman was in the wrong place at the wrong time. That's if the cave-in hadn't been an accident.

"True. There are some things we'll never know

the answer to. Which angle do we do in the play? Ruby Lewis and Duncan or Ruby Lewis and Wilson?" Her shoulders sagged. "I regret mentioning this stupid play."

"You didn't know a lot of this information when you proposed the idea."

"Still, it's a stupid idea. Not in the least bit romantic. It reads more like a murder mystery with tales of revenge and greed." She folded the papers and returned them to her pocket. "I say we go with the romantic angle and use Wilson, the man she went to meet."

"The man who survived."

"Exactly. Unfortunately, he's rarely mentioned. Other than the woman who told us about him at the diner, it's as if he didn't exist."

"I bet he perished, same as Lewis and Wilson. It shouldn't be hard to find a list of who died in that cave-in. It doesn't solve anything but our curiosity."

"I'm ready for this whole thing to be over. Let's get to work. The sooner the fourth gets here, the sooner we can put this all behind us."

The sooner she'd be gone. He wasn't sure how he felt about her leaving.

Chapter Twelve

After staying up too late working on the Fourth of July play Pressley had lost interest in, she rolled out of bed and shuffled to the shower. Once she woke up, she wanted to visit Myrtle at the library and dig up more information on her Colville relatives. If she had to be in limbo until fulfilling her obligations in Misty Hollow, she might as well do a bit of genealogy searching.

She showered, then dressed and settled in the chair by the window. River had work to do, so she'd be on her own for breakfast. She took a minute to check her voice mail. A message from a lawyer asking her to call him. A glance at the clock let her know she'd have to call after breakfast.

She gathered what she needed into her bag and drove to the diner, foregoing a walk. A piece of paper fluttered from under her windshield wiper. She'd remove it when she reached the diner.

Until her uncle's murderer was caught, she didn't want to be out alone. If the killer found out there was another direct descendant of the Colvilles, a target might be placed on her back.

She found a parking place several spots over from the door and climbed out. She pulled the paper from under her wiper. Stupid advertise—except this wasn't.

Hello, Cuz. Let's meet up someday. I'll be in touch.

Her hand trembled. The note came across as friendly, but she knew it to be anything but. This was a warning. She rushed inside the diner. "Just one today." She glanced over her shoulder as the hostess led her to a small table.

A few folks smiled and waved. Some still gave frosty stares, but those became fewer with each passing day. Most seemed to realize the effort she put into the Fourth of July celebration and her work at preserving the town's history, no matter how dark that history might be.

She peered over her menu at the other diners, focusing on the men. Most paid more attention to their food than her. Was one of them the killer? If only she could see their eyes close up.

"What can I get you?"

"Chocolate gravy and coffee, please." She smiled and handed over the unopened menu. "My favorite."

"I can tell." The girl smiled. "Be right up."

While she waited, she watched as a man in faded coveralls left the diner and approached her car. He placed something under the windshield wiper before strolling away.

Pressley jumped to her feet and darted outside. "Hey!"

The man ran, soon disappearing around the corner.

She removed the note.

I like chocolate gravy, too. Something we have in common.

Again, the note didn't sound threatening, but she knew differently and planned to pay a visit to the sheriff after breakfast. She contemplated sending River a text, then decided not to. If things were going to get more dangerous, the last thing she wanted to do was put him in harm's way. This was her family business, unfortunately. Hers to deal with alone.

She returned to the diner and scarfed down her breakfast before returning to her car and calling Uncle Frank's lawyer. "This is Pressley Hamilton returning your call."

"Very good, Miss Hamilton. I have your uncle's will. He's left everything to you. You can either come to my office to sign the papers or I can mail them to you, and you can have them signed and notarized. Everything is very straightforward."

"Please hold on to them. I should be returning to Memphis within the month." She now had a legitimate reason to return home. Why didn't she feel more pleased?

"That we can do. Please come in at your convenience. Aren't you interested in knowing the worth of what your uncle left you?"

"Not really."

"Let's just say that if you sell the business along with his bank account, you're set for life, young lady. Have a good day."

Pressley didn't care about the money. She didn't mind working for what she had. What would she do with all that money anyway?

She contemplated the land. Could she do something worthwhile with the place? Close down the mine and use the land to help the less fortunate? Definitely something to think about. She started the car and drove to the sheriff's office.

After fifteen minutes in the waiting room surrounded by an angry mother who claimed someone stole her son's bike, a man who'd imbibed a little too early, and another who screamed at the receptionist that he'd paid his ticket the previous month, Pressley was ushered into the sheriff's office.

"How can I help you, Miss Hamilton?"

"I've received these on my car." She filled him in on her discovery about her family and the fact that she'd witnessed the man leave the second note. "Unfortunately, I didn't see his face."

"Lots of men around here wear faded coveralls." He read the notes. "If not for the recent trouble around here, I wouldn't think anything of them."

"Me neither. That's why I brought them to you."

"Any idea who the man is that left you the notes?"

"No, sir, but I was told he could have a brown dot in the white of his eye. That it's a family trait among the men."

He quirked an eyebrow. "That right?"

"Do you know someone like that?" Hope leaped in her chest.

"I might. I'll definitely have my deputies keeping an eye out for such a person."

She didn't believe him. The look in his eyes told her he suspected who the killer was but determined to keep her from pursuing her own investigation. She offered a smile she was sure didn't reach her eyes.

"Thank you, Sheriff."

~

Now that Roy had spent some time putting fear in the heart of Pressley, it was time to mess with the cowboy. He'd be harder to get to, but Roy was a smart man. He'd find a way.

From his front window, he spotted the cursed cowboy's truck rumbling past. He grinned and grabbed his car keys from the hook near the door and his toolbox from under a nearby table. If he hurried, he might have a chance to stop the man for good.

He drove down Main Street a little faster than he should until he spotted the truck in front of the mercantile. His plan would be tricky, but if he hurried… He shoved the door to his truck open and, staying low, rushed toward the cowboy's truck.

Not seeing anyone paying him attention, he dropped to the asphalt and slid his upper body under the truck's carriage. One snip of his knife, and brake fluid dripped slowly into a puddle.

Roy grinned and scurried back to his own truck and drove away wishing he could see the aftermath for himself. It would be better if the cowboy had to drive down the mountain instead of up. If nothing else, the cowboy would get a good scare. A big enough one for him to back away from helping Pressley.

If that didn't work, he'd plan something bigger and better.

~

River hefted the last sack of grain into the bed of his truck. Since he needed to head into Harrisburg to pick up some engine parts, he'd volunteered to make the stop at the mercantile.

"Sorry I'm wanting to close up early," Fred said. "My grandkids are having a birthday party, and I promised to be there. Thankfully, it isn't scheduled to rain so the grain should be fine while you drive to Harrisburg and back."

"It's fine." He had wanted to make the mercantile stop on his way back, but it really wasn't that big of a deal. "Thanks for waiting around for me." He tipped his hat and climbed into his truck. Minutes later he honked and waved as he passed the sheriff's office and spotted Pressley exiting. Hopefully, everything was fine. He pressed the button on his console, "Call Pressley."

"Calling the mobile number for Pressley," the robotic voice said.

"Hey, River."

"Everything okay?" Once out of the main part of Misty Hollow, he increased his speed toward the interstate.

"Yeah. My new cousin has left me a couple of welcoming notes." She read them to him. "They don't sound threatening, but anyway, I think the sheriff knows a man with a brown spot in his eye."

River frowned. "Why do you think that?"

"A look he had, a gut feeling."

"I reckon if anyone would, he would. He didn't give you a clue?"

"Not a one. I'm going to ask Lucy. Don't know why I hadn't thought of that before. If this man lives in Misty Hollow, he's bound to have gone to the diner."

"That's a great idea. Let me know what you find out. And Pressley?"

"Yeah?"

"Don't go after him alone, please. Call the sheriff.

If you can't do that, then at least wait for me." He wasn't crazy about going after a killer, but if she did call him, he'd know she hadn't contacted the sheriff, and he could. "Promise me."

She sighed. "I promise."

He took the next exit onto the interstate. "Say it again."

She laughed. "I promise, River. I may be stubborn, but I'm not stupid."

"Good." He pressed the accelerator.

"I spoke to my uncle's lawyer. Turns out I'm going to be a wealthy woman."

"That's good news, right?"

"Maybe. Now I have to figure out what I'm going to do with my life. I've only known work."

He wanted to tell her to stay. Find a job here, but what would a woman with a high-executive job do in Misty Hollow? "You'll figure it out."

A semitruck pulled off an exit and swerved into River's lane. He hit the brake. The pedal went all the way to the floor. He pressed again. "Uh-oh."

"What?"

"I've lost my brakes." Not a good thing while careening down the interstate at eighty miles per hour.

"River! What are you going to do?"

"Find a place in the ditch to hit. Something soft, preferably."

"Stay on the line with me."

"Oh, darlin', I will." He yanked the steering wheel to avoid another car. So far, the sides of the road were too steep for him to plow into. All he had to do was keep control of the truck until the ground leveled out some. Then find a stand of saplings. "I've just passed mile marker 108. There's a swamp coming up that's muddy but not deep. I'm going there. Can you call me a ride?"

"Absolutely. I'll call you right back."

Horns blared as he shot across traffic into the bog. He jerked forward as the thick mud brought his truck to an abrupt stop. The seatbelt jerked. Airbags exploded. He shoved the bag away from him and worked on opening the door of the truck.

Vehicles stopped on the shoulder of the interstate. "You okay?" A man yelled through an open window as River shoved against his door.

"Good." He gave the man a thumbs-up and sank to his knees in the mud. With a squelch, he pulled his boots free, then removed them to plod in his socks to the interstate.

Cars stopped, but he waved them on, telling them he had help coming. With a grimace, he shoved his muddy feet back into his boots. He'd have a heck of a time getting them cleaned.

Half an hour later, a tow truck arrived. Once the mechanic freed his truck from the bog, River studied the undercarriage. He located the hole in his brake line right off.

Someone had wanted him harmed or worse.

Chapter Thirteen

In order for River to finish the jobs he had on the ranch, Pressley went to him. With only a few minor details left in the script for the Fourth of July skit, they could talk while he worked.

She drove up to the house just as Marilyn rang the cowbell to signal breakfast. Hooking her bag over her shoulder, she headed for the back door. River opened it as she stepped onto the deck.

"Good morning." A crease furrowed his brow. "Any more notes?"

"Not a one, thank goodness." She smiled and sniffed. "Good morning to you. I smell pancakes."

"Good sniffer. Mrs. White makes the fluffiest around."

"Hey, Pressley." Eric or Derrick—she still couldn't tell—tossed her a half wave as she entered the kitchen before returning to a quiet conversation with his twin.

Quiet. Hmm. Didn't that usually mean kids were up to something? Since no one else seemed overly concerned, she took the seat River pulled out for her.

"Thank you."

"Here you go." Mrs. White set a plate of pancakes in front of her.

"I can never eat all this." She stared at the short stack of eight.

"I'll finish what you don't eat." River grinned.

"That's my boy." Mrs. White clapped him on the shoulder on her way to serving the next man.

"She likes it when we eat a lot," he whispered, leaning close. His breath tickled the hair on Pressley's nape.

A pleasant shudder spread through her. "I'll, uh, definitely have some left for you." Mercy. Her hand shook as she reached for the syrup. Get your act together, girl. You'll be leaving soon. No entanglements. She had a future to figure out. But she sure was having mixed feelings about the caring man next to her.

"You okay?" Concern flickered in his eyes.

"Just thinking." She poured a liberal amount of syrup over her pancakes, then cut and bit into the fluffiest pancake she'd ever eaten. "Like a maple cloud. Yummy."

"Music to my ears." Mrs. White smiled.

"Boys, stop whispering, it's rude." Dylan Wyatt entered and sat at the end of the table. "Sorry, I'm late. Emails." He straightened when his plate of pancakes was set in front of him.

"No one waited." Mrs. White laughed. "As if anyone other than God Himself could make this bunch wait when food is sitting hot in front of them."

He chuckled. "Nice to see you again, Pressley. You've created quite the stir in town."

"I've been following your exploits." His wife, Dani, sat down to his right. "Putting together the history of this town is a great idea."

"It didn't start out that way." She glanced around the table. "I came here to purchase the Duncan land."

"Looks like that was taken care of for you." Dani smiled and buttered her pancakes before choosing powdered sugar instead of syrup. "Sorry about your uncle."

"Thank you." Appetite gone, she forced herself to take another bite.

One part of her couldn't wait until the Fourth of July came and went, so she could move on. The other part of her wanted to stay and see what might come of her friendship with River. Unless she was mistaken—which she doubted, considering her talent for assessing people—he cared for her as more than a friend. Maybe not as a romantic interest, at least not yet, but that could come. It probably would come if she mentioned staying. Why did life have to be so complicated?

"Folks are starting to like you," Dani said. "I can relate to that early distrust they have for newcomers, but your stepping up to do the Fourth of July celebration and write down the history have gone a long way toward helping the people welcome you."

Pressley nodded. She hadn't cared at first whether they liked her or not. Once the land was purchased, she'd have been long gone. Now, things had changed, and her mind became muddied. She didn't like the feeling. As a person who always knew the next step to take, uncertainty made her feel anxious—out of control.

The twins ate quickly and excused themselves, running outside with the dog, Monster, who had hidden under the table. Pressley flinched at the banging of the door.

After forcing down three of the pancakes, she slid her plate to River. "I'll wait for you on the back deck." She refilled her coffee and carried it outside with her.

The boys made a mad dash for the woods at the opposite end of the land. Their furtive glances over their shoulders alerted her to the fact they were probably up to no good. She set her coffee cup down on the patio table, placed her bag on one of the chairs, and followed them. If they were up to mischief, she could put a stop to it before someone got hurt. If their actions were innocent, then she'd taken a good morning walk while River finished eating.

Pressley longed for her snake leathers as she left the plowed fields and entered the recesses of the forest. Fortunately, a clear trail stretched in front of her, cutting through the trees. She should be able to spot a snake if one slithered across her path. Not to mention that the boys' clamoring up ahead would scare away almost anything. Smiling, she followed the noise.

The thick trees kept the morning from being too hot as the summer sun rose. Birds serenaded her. Why hadn't she taken time for a leisurely hike before now? All the cares and worries of the last few weeks slipped from her shoulders, washed away by the sound of a babbling brook to her right.

Just when she'd decided she'd gone far enough and would call out to the boys, she spotted them crawling under a barbed-wire fence. "Do tell me you aren't going to the mine." She planted her fists on her hips.

Instead of answering, they took off at a run.

With a sigh, Pressley followed and reached for the phone she kept in her back pocket. Her hand came up empty.

~

River stepped onto the back deck to no Pressley. Her cup and bag showed she'd been there. After glancing around at the outbuildings, he headed back into the house. "Anyone seen Pressley?"

"Maybe she's in the bathroom," Marilyn offered.

"No, I just came from there," Mrs. White said. "Unless she used the one upstairs."

River checked both bathrooms. No Pressley. She must be walking the grounds. It had taken him longer to eat than normal, and he'd gone over some of the week's chore list with Dylan. He carried her cold coffee from the back deck to the kitchen before setting off to look for her.

Pressley wasn't waiting for him in the barn or the corrals. The garage was empty except for the tractor waiting for repairs.

River removed his brown cowboy hat and ran his fingers through his hair before replacing the hat. She wasn't in the house, she wasn't in any of the outbuildings, and her car still sat where she'd parked it. There was also no sign of the boys or Monster.

His gaze moved to the woods. Could she have gone for a hike with them? He turned and headed in that direction wishing she would've waited for him. A stroll through the woods with her sounded like the perfect morning.

Putting his fingers to his lips, he let out a shrill whistle, then listened to see whether anyone responded. When no answering call came, he did it again and continued down the path.

A few footprints, some obviously the boys', then what looked like the print of a sandal showed in the dirt near the edge of the trail where the shadows kept the sun from drying the ground quickly after the rains a couple of days ago. At least he was on the right track.

When he reached the creek, he stopped to listen, then whistled again. Still not hearing anything, he frowned. Shouldn't he hear the boys by now? He was nearing the edge of the property, and he knew for a fact they'd been forbidden to leave the property until the man shooting at people was caught.

He shook his head and continued. His steps halted at the sight of something lying in the path ahead of him. Taking a deep breath, he moved forward and retrieved Pressley's phone. His heart dropped. She never went anywhere without her phone.

"Pressley! Eric! Derrick!" When no response came, he turned and sprinted back the way he'd come. He barged into Dylan's office. "Pressley and the boys are not on the property. I found her phone in the woods." He set it on his boss's desk.

Dylan lunged to his feet and pulled a handgun from the top drawer of his desk. "How long have they been gone?"

"The boys left breakfast about eight. Pressley right after."

"Okay. Ring the bell to summon the others. Meet near the barn." He rushed from the room.

River moved to the front porch and clanged the cowbell before heading to the bunkhouse for his gun. If the boss thought a weapon was needed, then he wouldn't go empty handed. A few minutes later, he joined the others in front of the barn and filled them in on what little he knew.

"I want some of you on horseback, the others on foot," Dylan said. "Split up and check the road and the woods. They have over an hour start on us. River, you and me are in the woods."

"Yes, sir." He fell into step beside Dylan while the others rushed for their horses.

"I haven't spanked the twins in a long time, but if I find one toe on the Duncan land, I'm going to blister their backsides." Dylan marched at a quick pace.

River wanted to tell him the boys wouldn't disobey, but he knew different. The rascals were always testing the boundaries. He also knew his boss spoke out of anger and worry, not that he'd actually whup the boys. "I'm sure they're okay. Pressley is probably with them. They could be showing her their new hangout since the mine is off limits."

"Right." Dylan shot him a disbelieving glance. "For their bottoms' sake, you'd better be right. Who am I kidding? They're too old for a whuping even if I wanted to give them one. They'll be grounded until they're eighteen."

"How long do you want to wait before calling the sheriff's department?" River's boss's temper needed tamping.

"Let's find out where they've gone first."

River nodded. "I don't like the idea that Pressley left her phone behind."

"Me neither, but she could have simply dropped it."

They kept tracking up to the barbed-wire fence. "Looks like they went through."

Dylan's features hardened. "Call the sheriff. We're following them."

~

Things had gone better than Roy had hoped. Luring the boys with promises of a buried treasure had also brought him Pressley. Roy slapped his knee.

He'd wanted the boys to lure her into giving herself up, but he hadn't planned on her following them. Things were going even better than planned.

Staying to the shadows of the forest and using trees and thick foliage as cover, he followed them across the Duncan fields toward the mine. Pressley hadn't caught up to the twins but complained out loud about the danger of snakes.

Foolish woman. There were far more dangerous things in the woods.

He wished she'd move faster. He had no doubt the cowboy would find her missing and come looking. Before that happened, he needed her to go deep into the mine where her "accident" could happen. If the boys perished with her, then they were simply collateral damage and would add to the horror stories pertaining to the Duncan mine.

The eerie stories about the mine worked in his favor. The resort he planned to build would be filled with people hoping to see the ghosts of those who had perished.

He rubbed his hands and grinned. Things were going exactly the way he wanted them to.

Chapter Fourteen

The urge to go after the boys swept stronger than Pressley's need to go look for her phone. She no longer had any doubt that the boys were headed for the mine. Why? Their father had explicitly forbidden them to.

With her heart in her throat over the threat of snakes in the knee-high grass, she continued toward the boys' destination. When she found them, she'd throttle them! Then, she'd gladly hand them over to their father so he could do the same. If she died from a snake bite, she'd do more than throttle them.

As she neared the mine entrance, the twins' conversation grew louder. She crept closer, doing her best not to step on a twig and alert them to her presence. She failed. The snap sounded as loud as a gunshot.

"What was that?" One of the boys asked.

"An animal."

"Could be the shooter."

"Nah. It's too early in the day for the shooter. He's always shot at people close to suppertime."

Weird logic, but Pressley grinned as she moved

aside the brush covering the entrance and stepped inside. "What are the two of you doing here? Where is the crime-scene tape?"

They whipped around, the paper they'd been holding between them ripped in half. "Right through the X!" One of them glared.

Pressley put her hands on her hips. "I asked you a question."

"We're looking for treasure." They scowled and held the ripped pieces of the paper together.

"Where did you get the map?" She peered over their shoulders.

"In the barn. Someone tried to hide it in the hay, but we're too smart for that."

"Of course, you are. Who's who?" She wagged her finger between them. "Don't lie. This is important."

"I'm Eric." He wore a red tee shirt. "He's Derrick." In blue.

Pressley nodded. "Let's go before your father kills all three of us." She started to step outside when another twig snapped, then she heard the sound of a rock falling downhill. "Shh." She peered out to see a man climbing up toward them. "Someone is coming. Is there another way out?"

Eric nodded. "According to the map, we head down that tunnel, then take the first right. Derrick, pull out your flashlight."

This was not good at all. Who knew what dangers lurked in the dark recesses of the mine?

"Keep the light off until absolutely necessary." Maybe the man outside didn't know they were there. "Go. Quickly now." She gave the boys a gentle shove. "Stay quiet."

She had to run to keep up with them. When it became too dark to see, she told Derrick to turn on the flashlight. "How far until we turn right?" She whispered.

"I don't know." Eric glanced over his shoulder. "The map doesn't give us feet or yards. Just dashes. Don't worry, Pressley. We've been chased by a killer before. We're experts."

"Yeah," Derrick added. "Just stay close to us, and you'll be fine. It'll all be worth it once we find the treasure."

Who were these two? Children shouldn't be so lackadaisical about danger. Her heart threatened to beat free as they stumbled along looking for a treasure that most likely didn't exist. It occurred to her that the map was a trap to lure her to the mine. Whoever left it knew she'd follow them.

What if one of the cowhands had spotted the boys? Then, the killer would've come up with a new plan. It was as simple as that.

"Do either of you have a cell phone?" She asked.

"No. Dad said we aren't old enough yet. He doesn't always listen to us. Maybe once we get out of here, he'll change his mind."

A thud sounded behind them.

Pressley whipped around. Inky blackness obscured anything or anyone that might be following. "Shh." She motioned the boys onward.

They came to a fork and turned right. Something nagged at her. If they were lured into the mine with a false treasure map, then the person responsible would send them in the wrong direction. "Wait. Go left instead."

"But the map says—"

"Trust me on this. The map is a fake. Turn left."

Grumbling, the two did as she said. If they were lucky, the man following them would assume they turned right and head in that direction.

"We have no idea where we're going now," Eric grumbled. "What if you're wrong?"

"Then I'll live with that mistake for the rest of my life." She'd learned a long time ago to trust her instincts and didn't plan on stopping now.

"We don't know you well enough to trust you." Derrick turned, shining the light in her eyes, blinding her.

"We need to be quiet." She pushed the light out of her face. "If I'm wrong, we'll come back and do things your way. Okay?"

The boys glanced at each other, then nodded before turning and continuing down the tunnel.

Curses echoed in the distance.

Pressley pushed against the twins. "Run. We've made him angry." Which meant she was right. The man had intended to trap them.

Their footsteps thundered across the packed dirt of the tunnel. Pressley's breathing came in gasps so loud she felt certain the man chasing them could hear. When they came to another fork, she grabbed the boys' arms. "Listen."

A faint cool breeze came from their right. "This way." She took each of them by the hand and continued to run.

An explosion shook the ground under their feet. Her legs gave way and she fell, taking the boys down with her.

~

River stopped as a plume of dust rose in the air after a hollow boom. "What was that?"

"An explosion or a cave-in." Dylan sprinted across the pastureland. As he ran, he yelled into his cell phone that all hands were needed at the Duncan mine ASAP. "Bring horses and side-by-sides. Now!"

River's heart lodged in his throat. His legs threatened to give way. Pressley and the twins were in there. He knew they were. Had the Duncan mine claimed more lives? The life of the woman he could envision a future with? *Please, God, no.* Sweat was dripping down his back by the time they arrived at the mine entrance. Together, he and Dylan barged inside.

Dust clogged the air. River pulled the neckline of his shirt over his nose. "We need to find the cave-in. Is there another exit?"

"No idea." Dylan pulled a bandana from his pocket and tied it around his nose and mouth. "Got a light?"

"Just my phone."

"Me, too. Use yours first. When your battery is dead, we'll use mine if help hasn't arrived."

River nodded and turned on the flashlight option on his phone before leading the way down the tunnel. "Pressley!"

"Eric! Derrick!" Dylan's muffled voice echoed off the walls.

Fear choked River more than the dust thickening the air, but he had to persevere. "Pressley!"

A gunshot rang out.

River and Dylan dove to the ground.

More gunshots had them covering their heads as

dirt and pebbles rained down on their heads.

Footsteps thundered toward them.

A man charged from the darkness, leaped over them, and darted from the mine.

"Look for the boys." River jumped to his feet and gave chase, pulling his gun from the holster at his waist.

"Don't shoot him," Dylan said. "I need answers first."

No promises. If the man didn't tell him where Pressley and the boys were, then his life would be forfeited.

"Stop or I'll shoot!" River fired his weapon in the air. Gunfire was the immediate response. The man he chased would have no qualms of shooting him, especially since he'd possibly brought the mine down on the heads of Pressley and the twins.

River's mouth dried. He refused to think that way. Pressley and the twins were fine. They might not even be in the mine. Maybe the man hadn't set an explosive. He could have simply been there during the cave-in and dashed out to keep from being buried. Then why fire at River and the sheriff?

River left the cave and stopped behind an oak tree big enough to shield him. Gun at the ready, he peered out to try and spot the man's location. A squirrel scolded him from the branches over his head.

A bullet carved a chunk of bark from the trunk. River's cheek burned where the bark hit. Taking a deep breath, he stepped from his cover and started firing.

The roar of an engine approached from behind him. When Maverick appeared behind the wheel of a side-by-side, River waved him on. "That way. Caucasian wearing an army green hoodie and camouflage pants."

Maverick gave him a thumbs-up and roared past.

River dashed back to the mine. He couldn't see more than a glimmer of light down the tunnel to prove Dylan was still inside. "Find anything, Boss?"

A few seconds later, Dylan joined him. "The boys' footprints go in both directions, but then they turn around. That's where the cave-in must have happened. The prints go farther down a different tunnel. I think the three of them found a way out. They're not in the tunnel that's blocked."

"Let's go see." With a prayer in his heart that Dylan was right, River followed him at a run.

They continued on until a sliver of outside light greeted them. A breeze showed them the way to the opening.

River burst out first. His body weakened to the point of almost collapsing. Pressley and the boys sat on boulders, passing around a water bottle.

"River!" Pressley jumped up and into his arms. "There was an explosion."

He pressed his arms around her. "We know. I chased the man responsible but lost him. Maverick is out looking for him."

Dylan dropped down on one knee, clasping his sons to his chest.

River stepped back and cupped Pressley's face. "I was so scared."

"Me too, for a while. The boys had found a treasure map in the barn. I think it was a trap to lure them out here. I was the target, but that person was willing to take the chance I'd follow them out here." Her eyes widened. "He would've killed all three of us in that mine."

He turned at the sound of hoofprints to see the other cowboys ride up.

"We brought extras so these three could ride back." Ryder slid from his horse and brought two from the end of the line.

"Thanks, man." Now that the danger had passed and the adrenaline dissipated, exhaustion weighed his limbs. Riding sounded a heck of a lot better than walking at this point.

Dylan put the two boys on a horse, then swung up behind them, leaving the other horse for River and Pressley. "See everyone back at the ranch." He clicked his tongue and headed his horse toward the ranch.

"What about the man who followed us?" Pressley asked as River helped her onto the other horse.

"If Maverick doesn't get him, he'll be back." River swung up behind her. When the man returned, he'd have to face River's wrath. He wrapped his left arm around Pressley, a gesture that felt as natural as breathing, and his right hand gripped the reins. "All I care about right now is getting you home and taken care of."

"That sounds wonderful." She leaned back against him.

He closed his eyes and breathed deep of her—dust, sweat, and the floral scent of her shampoo—he was more grateful than he could ever remember.

For now.

Chapter Fifteen

How could she have escaped? Roy tossed a duffel bag into the back of his truck, then climbed into the driver's seat and sped away. He'd stayed too long. Someone would identify him soon.

It didn't matter. He had a plan to improve Misty Hollow once he came into what was his. The town would be the tourist destination of the state. The country! The people would be indebted to him because of his generosity.

For now, he'd have to hole up somewhere until he came up with the next step in his plan. Oh, he definitely intended to continue his harassment, keeping his cousin on her toes. If he got lucky, she'd walk away and leave the land to him without a fight. If not, he needed all of his resources in case they had to fight in court, which he'd avoid at all possible. If someone identified him as the one shooting at people who came near the mine, there'd be no court date. Nothing but a jail cell for him.

He drummed his fingers on the steering wheel to the tune of an old 1980s hit. He could do this. Everything would fall into place. All he needed was an alibi for the last couple of weeks. His mother would vouch for him. He'd go to her. She only lived an hour away—not too far that he couldn't work on his plan for Misty Hollow from her place.

He flicked on his turn signal and took the next exit off the interstate.

~

"We have a person of interest in the shooting at the mine." Sheriff Westbrook removed his hat, remaining on the front porch. "After finding out about the brown spot in the white of the eye, we narrowed it down to Roy Hyatt."

Pressley grinned as hope lifted. "Did you take him in?"

"He isn't at his place. Since he lives off a ways from any main road, his closest neighbor is a mile away, so there's no one to report whether or not he's been around. We should have a next of kin soon."

"I'm the next of kin." She lowered into a deck chair, wishing River hadn't gone to town for automobile parts. The proverbial rug under her feet was unraveling, and she could use his arm to remain standing.

"Hopefully, we can find someone closer." The sheriff smiled. "We'll get him, Miss Hamilton. Whether it's Roy or not, we always get our man...or woman." He glanced around them. "Glad to see you're staying at the ranch until this is over. The motel is too secluded."

"River insisted after the mine incident."

"Good." He replaced his hat. "We'll keep you posted, ma'am. Try not to go anywhere alone."

"Thank you." Like that did any good yesterday. She had the twins with her, and the man who killed her uncle still came after her. If he'd caught up with them, she wouldn't have been the only casualty.

He tapped his fingers against his hat brim and returned to his car. She waited until he drove away, then went back into the house and upstairs to the room she'd be staying in for who knew how long.

With a sigh, she sat in a cushy chair near the window. Idleness was not her friend. She'd gone through all the papers on the town's history, read the journal, and completed the plans for the Fourth of July celebration. Until her uncle's affairs were in order and she knew what her future held, her life hung in limbo.

Maybe she could be of help in the kitchen. She pushed to her feet and returned downstairs.

"Everything okay?" Mrs. White glanced over from where she washed the morning dishes.

"Yes. Need help?"

"Sure. Grab a towel. Marilyn ran into town for some groceries." She narrowed her eyes. "You look fretful."

"Just wondering how to fill my time."

"We can always use your help here." She smiled, handing Pressley a plate. "How's the history coming?"

"I've read through it all."

"Why not write it down? Put it in a book? There are plenty of folks around here that would be happy to purchase such a thing."

"Really?" Plate dried, she started a stack on the counter. "I primarily did the research to find out more about the mine."

"Well, people around here are interested in those old stories, especially about the mine. I say, write a book. You've no end of research available at the diner."

She chuckled. "I found that out." Excitement started to well. "Maybe I will. It would definitely give me something to do until this person is caught. Do you know a Roy Hyatt?"

"Oh, sure. He's a local yard and handyman, just like his father. Well, not his biological father." Her eyes twinkled. "He's illegitimate, you know."

"I've discovered that."

"He's a nice enough guy. A bit of a loner. Some say he's a bit…simple." She tapped her head. "I've not met him, but I've seen him around. Never gave me a lick of trouble."

"What color are his eyes?"

"No idea." She frowned. "That's a strange question."

"Just wondering." Pressley put the stack of dried dishes in the cupboard. "I think I'll grab my laptop and sit out on the deck to start this book. Thank you for the suggestion."

Five minutes later, she sat at the patio table with her laptop and notes. The summer sun warmed her shoulders. A horse nickered from the paddock. The day couldn't be more peaceful.

She shoved aside the worry over Roy Hyatt and focused instead on where to start writing. A book would be a different style of writing than the reports she was used to, but she could do this. Mrs. White was right. It would occupy Pressley's time and keep her from doing something stupid, like setting a trap.

"Here's some coffee. You've been out here for over an hour." Mrs. White set a cup in front of her and raised the table umbrella.

"Wow. It doesn't seem that long. All I'm doing

right now is organizing my notes."

"I'd advise you to find out who wants the Duncan land in those pages, but I suspect you already know."

Pressley glanced up. "Word does travel around this ranch."

"It sure does. Especially when two rowdy boys eavesdrop on your conversation with the sheriff." She patted Pressley's shoulder. "Don't worry. I've warned them to keep the man's name to themselves."

~

River wasn't crazy about leaving Pressley, but she wasn't alone on the ranch—not by a long shot. The other hands would keep an eye on her as well as he could.

He hoisted a truck battery into the back of his truck and turned as the sheriff pulled up beside him. "Howdy."

"Mornin'." The sheriff told him of his visit with Pressley earlier. "Turns out Roy Hyatt has been at his mother's in Harrisburg for the last month. Taking care of her, she said, so we're back to the drawing board."

"I guess there isn't anyone else around who has those eyes?" River leaned on his truck.

"Not that I know of, but we'll keep looking and asking around. As I told Miss Hamilton, we'll get him."

River nodded. When the sheriff drove away, he climbed into his truck and headed back to the ranch. He raked his mind for a Roy Hyatt and came up empty. It didn't matter. The man wasn't the one they were looking for if he was taking care of his mother.

Which put them at square one.

He took the turn that led up the mountain. If he were to start hanging around the mine without Pressley joining him, he might be able to draw the man out. If he didn't get shot. There were a lot of ifs in that scenario.

It wasn't River the man wanted; it was Pressley. Somehow, River needed to catch the man before he achieved his goal. That was the only sure way to keep Pressley safe. But, if she found out what he was up to, she'd insist on helping, or worse, going after the man alone.

He pulled in front of the garage and glanced toward the main house. Pressley sat on the deck, laptop and papers in front of her. After carrying the new truck battery into the garage, River strode her way. "Hey."

She glanced up and smiled. "Hey, yourself."

He propped his booted right foot on the step. "The sheriff said he stopped by."

"Yep." She told him of their conversation which was the same as his minus the man visiting his mother.

He filled her in. "What are you working on?"

"Mrs. White said that folks around here would be interested in a book about Misty Hollow, so I'm writing one." She shrugged. "It gives me something to do."

"What would be really nice is if you found something in those papers we missed before. Something that gives you the edge over this man—"

"Something that draws him out?" She arched a brow. "Yes, that would be nice. I'm pretty sure anything of that nature would be in my uncle's files, which I can't access yet."

"Any idea when?" He didn't mind her digging as long as it wasn't in the mine.

"Any day now, according to his lawyer." She stretched. "I need to take a break."

"It's almost lunchtime. Want to grab some

sandwiches and go for a horseback ride? We won't go far. I know what the sheriff said."

Her smile widened. "A picnic sounds wonderful."

"Be right back." Ten minutes later, his face heated from Mrs. White's snide looks and murmurs about another cowboy biting the dust. He carried a backpack stuffed with food from the kitchen.

She wasn't too far off. He did like Pressley—more than *like* her if he were honest—and he'd spend as much time with her as possible in order to find a way to keep her in Misty Hollow.

After saddling two horses and securing the pack, he led the horses to the deck where Pressley awaited him.

"I'm not a good rider."

"Not a problem." He whistled for Ryder who came and led one of the horses back to the barn. "We'll ride together." Something he preferred anyway, especially after riding behind her the day before.

They rode without talking through the woods until they reached the creek. He made sure they stayed on the ranch and in sight of the main house. If trouble came, he knew the area well enough to find them a place to hide. He slid from the horse and helped Pressley to the ground. "How about that patch of moss over there? It'll be soft."

"Perfect." She headed to the water's edge.

He sat beside her and opened the pack. Resting on top was a single red rose. He laughed and handed it to Pressley. "Mrs. White's not-so-subtle hint."

Pressley's cheeks pinkened as she breathed in the scent. "How sweet."

Dunce. He should've said the rose was from him

as the ranch cook had meant it to be. He handed Pressley a sandwich. "BLT with cream cheese instead of mayo."

"Sounds delicious." She set the rose next to her, her sharp gaze on his face. "Why didn't you say the rose was from you?"

"Did you want me to?"

"I…yes."

"Then the rose is from me."

"But just as much of a surprise." She tilted her head.

"Yep." He laughed and tucked her hair over her shoulder. "Yesterday, when I found out you were missing, the bottom dropped out of my world. Then, when I heard the explosion, my heart shattered. I can't imagine a world without you in it."

Her eyes shimmered like the pools in the creek beside them. "I feel the same way, but I can't commit to anything. Not right now. Too many things are unsettled."

"Then, I'll be content with now." He cupped the back of her head and pulled her close, claiming her lips with his.

Softly, tenderly, she returned his kiss. A slight moan in her throat intensified his response until they were both breathless. He pulled back and smiled. "Yes, ma'am. I'll be content with now."

For now.

Chapter Sixteen

Pressley headed for her car, only to be called back by River. She pivoted to face him. "I'm only going to the post office."

"Guess I'm going there, too." He wiped his hands on a greasy rag.

"I'll only be gone thirty minutes."

"Sheriff's orders. You aren't to go anywhere alone." He shoved the rag into the back pocket of his jeans. "I'll drive."

Of course, he would. She sighed and climbed into the passenger seat. She loved him—she could admit that now—but she also needed alone time. Something in short supply on a bustling ranch.

"Why are you mad?" He turned the key in the ignition.

"I'm not mad." She clicked her seatbelt into place.

"Okay?" He didn't look convinced. "What's at the post office?" He turned the truck around and headed down the mountain.

"My uncle's files. I found something interesting in the journal and noticed the last page had been glued to the back cover. Behind that, I discovered a letter—a rather disturbing one about a man named Hyatt."

He frowned. "It can't be our Roy. Someone else?"

She shrugged. "This man had a big grudge against the Duncans. He wasn't involved in that fateful poker game, but he still thought the land and the mine belonged to him."

"Who wrote this letter?"

"The long-ago Duncan. Obviously, he didn't want it to be part of his journal but maybe hoped someone would find it someday." She shifted slightly in her seat. "I don't think Colville caused that cave-in, River; I think Hyatt did."

"To get rid of the competition?"

She nodded. "And now, his kin doesn't want that kind of information to get out. It would sully the name of Hyatt. Didn't you say Roy was well-liked in town?"

"Yes, but he's been at his mother's."

"Mothers often lie to protect their child."

"You would make a great investigative reporter. Maybe that should be your next career."

She laughed. "No schooling."

"I bet the local paper would hire you. What are your dreams?"

Pressing her lips together, she stared out the window for a moment, then said softly, "To make a difference. I really wasn't doing that working for Hamilton Enterprises."

"What will you do with the company?"

"Sell it, maybe." She shrugged. "I guess it's time to start seriously thinking about my future."

He reached over and took her hand. "I hope that future includes Misty Hollow."

She couldn't promise, but her heart felt the same as his. Could she make her home here? Find something fulfilling to do with her life? She glanced at River. Something that included him? Maybe. Hopefully.

"Want to grab lunch while we're in town?" He gave her hand a squeeze, then returned it to the steering wheel.

"That sounds great." The people of Misty Hollow had slowly come to accept her. Maybe she could make a home there. She needed to figure out how to make a difference if she were to stay.

River drove past the post office and parked in front of the diner. They headed to their favorite table by the window.

Pressley perused the specials written in chalk on a board as they passed. Chicken fried steak. Too heavy for a noon meal. She'd go for a simple salad.

Leaving her menu lying unopened on the table, she brought the subject of the mine up again. "Is quartz really that lucrative? I mean…it isn't gold."

He frowned for a minute, then his eyes widened. "Diamonds. It has to be. This state is known for its diamonds."

"That makes a lot more sense." Her heart raced. Could it be? "I haven't found anything that mentions diamonds."

"Maybe I'm wrong, but it's worth digging, no pun intended." He winked.

She laughed. "Who could we ask?"

"The library would be a good place to start, then ask some of the old-timers, I guess. Someone has to have heard a rumor passed down through their family." He studied those in the diner. A few minutes later, he motioned an elderly man over. "Got a minute, Herb?"

"Got lots of them, God willing." He gave a toothless grin. "Want more history on this town?"

"Yes, sir."

"Ever hear about diamonds at the Duncan mine?" Pressley asked.

"Someone found a diamond once. Just one. Only a couple of carats big and already cut. Only an idiot would think the Duncan mine was a diamond mine. No, I reckon someone lost the setting out of their ring."

"That's it?" Disappointment squelched her excitement.

"Sorry to disappoint you, but folks have looked and looked. Not a single diamond other than that one."

"Are there still people who think there might be diamonds in there?" River asked.

"The world is full of fools, isn't it? I reckon there's one or two. My coffee's getting cold."

"Thank you for your time." Pressley's shoulders sagged as the man returned to his seat. "It was a good idea even if it didn't pan out."

River ordered a burger when the server stopped at their table, then returned his attention to Pressley. "I still think someone might believe the rumor. There is money in quartz, though. Oh…"

"What?"

"There's money in opening the mine to tourists to dig for their own quartz crystals. I bet that's it. Your uncle wanted that land for a tourist destination, right? I bet he was going to open the mine to the resort's guests."

"You might have just hit the nail on the head." She grinned. "Good job. If that was his plan, it'll be in the files waiting for me at the post office." They were finally going to solve the mystery of the Duncan mine. Pressley couldn't help but feel a certain amount of sadness at the thought. Once they solved the mystery, she finished writing the book, and the Fourth of July celebration was over, she had a very big decision to make. She prayed she would make the right one.

After lunch, River drove her to the post office and waited in the truck while she went inside. The postmaster handed her a box the size of a large photo album. She signed for it and returned to the truck where she placed the box behind her seat. Pressley couldn't wait to return to the ranch and dig into her uncle's files.

~

While Pressley was in the post office, River thought more about the mine and the Duncan land. He knew an old logging-truck road ran along the back end of the property. Logic told him the shooter got in and out that way in order to avoid detection. He explained his theory to Pressley when she returned. "Want to take a drive? We can't go to the mine, but we might be able to find out something by making the drive down that road."

"Sure. If we see tracks, I can take photos. Maybe we'll find a vehicle the tracks match. But, I'm guessing the sheriff's department already did that."

"True, but they might've missed something." It never hurt to have a fresh set of eyes look over things.

Half an hour later, he drove off the highway onto a rarely used dirt road overgrown with weeds. A vehicle had driven there recently, flattening the weeds and grass. Proof number one. Since the road was on government land and rarely used except during deer season, he concluded it had to be the shooter. He pulled to the side of the road. "Want to wander around? We're on government land as long as we don't cross the fence."

"Sure. Oh, look." A flock of turkeys moved in front of them.

"They always know when turkey season's over." He chuckled and shoved open his door.

"So, we don't have to worry about a hunter mistaking us for game." She climbed from the truck. "I'll start here on this side of the road. The weeds aren't as tall, which means it's easier to watch for snakes."

Pressley and her fear of snakes.

He reversed directions and headed back down the road rather than crossing over. River doubted they'd find anything since it hadn't rained in days, but he wanted to prolong the time spent with Pressley before he returned to dirty-engine work and she buried herself in her uncle's files. Call him selfish.

He smiled to see her inching along the edge of the road ahead of him, her head down, concentrating on where she put her feet. The crunch of gravel alerted him to an approaching vehicle. He whipped around.

A battered pickup stopped a few yards away from them, its engine idling. River could make out the form of the driver. When the man didn't make a move to greet them or get out of the truck, River started back to the truck.

"Pressley, get back in the truck. Now."

"River—"

"Now."

"But there's a snake by my foot."

He stifled a curse, something he only did on the

rare occasion that danger reared in all directions. "Move back real slow." He reached her, then slowed down, his heart hammering in his throat.

"I'm scared. Where's your gun?"

"It's in the truck." He didn't think he'd need it. Keeping his eye on the idling truck, he hurried back toward his vehicle and grabbed his gun, then walked toward the mystery driver.

"Who is that, River?" she yelled to him. Just then the door closed behind him. He didn't dare take his eyes of the driver ahead, but he blew out a breath of relief that she had made it safely inside.

Just then a gun aimed straight at him from the truck's window.

"Get down, Pressley!"

The gun rang out. The first shot got him in the shoulder, spinning him like a top. The second shot in the side dropped him to his knees.

Shots rang out from behind him.

The shooter spun gravel backing away and disappeared down the road.

Fire burned through River. His blood soaked into the dirt under him. Spots swam in front of his eyes.

Pressley kneeled next to him. "What do I do? I don't have phone service."

"Radio in the glove compartment. Call the ranch. Someone will come."

"I don't want to leave you."

"I'm bleeding, sweetheart. You're coming right back. Where did you learn to shoot like that?"

"Uncle Frank. But, I'm not very good." She darted away.

Maybe not, but she'd frightened the shooter away.

As he closed his eyes, all he could think about was how angry Sheriff Westbrook was going to be because the two of them had gone investigating. He wouldn't care that it wasn't on private property. All he'd see was that River had gotten shot.

"They're sending a side-by-side." She pressed a handful of napkins to his waist. "I hate blood." She gagged.

"Please do not vomit on me." He chuckled, then hissed through the pain.

"I promise not to." She smiled through her tears. "But you have to promise me not to die."

"I'll do my best."

He must've passed out because the next thing he heard was the rumble of an engine. He turned his head as Maverick cut the barbed-wire fence in order to drive the side-by-side through.

"I'll repair it later," he said. "It's a shorter distance across the Duncan land. Man, the boss is spitting bullets." He helped River to his feet. "What do you want to do about your truck?"

"Leave it. Pressley is coming with us."

He nodded. "I'll send someone back for it." He settled River into the front passenger seat, leaving the small back seat for Pressley. "Hold on, ma'am. It's going to be a rough ride. River, you might want to bite down on this." He handed him a strap of leather.

The ride back to the ranch was nothing short of hell.

Chapter Seventeen

Pressley hovered in the doorway to one of the guest rooms as Mrs. White fussed over River as if he were a baby, but Pressley wanted to be the one to give him water and a pain pill, to check his bandages, and watch him as he slept.

It had been two days since he'd been shot. Two days of fearing the worst as a fever raged in his body. Now, he was home from the hospital, and she couldn't get within a foot of him.

When Mrs. White left because River appeared to have fallen asleep, his eyes opened, and he smiled. "Come here." He held out his right hand.

"I'm not sure your nurse will approve." Pressley took a step forward.

"Who cares? I want you near me."

"Will I hurt you if I sit beside you?" She eyed the sofa.

"No. Just go slow."

She took his hand and perched on the edge of the bed. "Are you really okay? The doctors said you will be better now that the fever is passed."

"I'm going to be fine. It hurts like the dickens, and the ride back to the ranch in the side-by-side did more harm than good since it jostled the bullet in my side around a bit, but it's all good now."

"While you've been in the hospital, I've been doing some digging." She smoothed his hair away from his face. "Looks like we might have a romantic triangle back in the day. Not with Duncan, but with Lewis, Colville, and Hyatt. According to a old newspaper report, Hyatt professed his undying devotion to Lewis, who publicly rejected him."

"That's a motive for murder." He rubbed his thumb across the back of her hand.

She nodded. "People have killed for less, and this not only involved rejection, but also humiliation." She sighed. "I'm not sure the people of Misty Hollow will like that tidbit of history."

"Sure, they will. People love a tragic romance. Look at *Romeo and Juliet.*"

"Do we have us a scholarly cowboy?" She tilted her head.

"I haven't read anything like that since high school." He laughed, then grimaced. "And that was only because I had to."

"I love to read. Can't imagine not reading." She leaned forward and placed a kiss on his forehead. "I'd better let you sleep before Mrs. White has my head. If you need me, I'll be on the deck writing."

He pulled her closer. "A kiss on the forehead is for babies." His eyes darkened. "I'm not in so much pain that you can't give me a real kiss."

Her face heated as she pressed her lips to his, her eyes drifting closed. She snapped them open when Mrs.

White cleared her throat. "I was just leaving." Pressley giggled, gave River another quick kiss, then rushed from the room like a teenager caught necking.

Outside, she settled at the patio table. The twins played fetch with the dog, Monster, filling the air with laughter until a van full of day-camping students parked out front.

Pressley contemplated taking her writing inside to avoid the noise that was sure to come, but she decided against it. The book she was writing was their history, same as their parents'. Their laughs and shouts might be just the muse she needed.

Her fingers flew across the keyboard as she started putting the notes she'd collected into some semblance of order. Once they were all typed in, she'd go back through and turn them into an actual book. She hoped.

An email popped up on her screen from an unknown address. She finished the paragraph she was writing, then switched screens.

Don't think you and the cowboy are out of danger. You should never have stuck your nose where it didn't belong. You'll regret digging into the history of my mine.

She wanted to respond that the mine was as much hers as his, but she decided to ignore the email until she had time to talk to River about it. Emails couldn't harm either of them. No one could get to them while they were on the ranch. They were safe for the time being.

Her gaze lifted to the trees at the far end of the property. Such a beautiful place, yet there were so many places for danger to hide in wait. The outbuildings provided her protection from anyone who might want to take a shot at her as she sat on the deck. Still, her skin prickled.

With a groan, she packed up and moved to the dining room table—a formal room hardly used that would provide her with some privacy and quiet. So much for the visiting children being her muse.

Another ding signaled another email. She jabbed the keyboard to open the message.

Once you're out of the way, I can move forward with my plans.

Leave Misty Hollow now or face the consequences.

Coward. Tell me to my face, she typed, then backspaced and deleted the message. She refused to give him the satisfaction of a response.

"If you type any harder, you're going to need a new keyboard." Mrs. White entered the room. "River is asking for you. The man is bored and wants to know how the book is coming. Despite my misgivings, he's moved into the living room."

"Thank you." More than happy to close her laptop and avoid any more messages, she leaped to her feet and rushed into the living room.

River lay propped up on the sofa, the television remote in his hand. He faced her and clicked off the TV. "Thank goodness. I'm about to lose my mind."

"You're supposed to be sleeping."

"I've slept enough. How is the book coming?"

"It's coming." She told him about the emails.

~

Rage boiled his blood. It wasn't enough the crazed fool had shot him not once but twice, but now he'd harassed Pressley via email. "How did he get your email address?"

"It's listed on the Hamilton Enterprises website. It isn't hard to find." She sat on the sofa next to him. "Should I tell the sheriff? There isn't much the man can do with emails, except maybe track the IP address, and I'm sure whoever is sending them will have thought of that."

"The sheriff can add this latest harassment to the list." His fingers curled so tight around the remote that his knuckles ached. They had to put an end to this. Tomorrow was the Fourth of July celebration. Anything could happen, and here he lay on the sofa like a beached whale. He was worthless if trouble came.

"I'll call him." She pulled her phone from the pocket of her skirt and made the call. When she hung up, she rose to her feet. "I need to go print out the emails. Be right back."

He nodded and forced himself into a sitting position. Doctor's orders or not, he intended on being at the celebration tomorrow. Someone needed to keep an eye on Pressley who would be flitting from one thing to another throughout the day. The only time she'd be still would be in the evening during the fireworks.

He'd planned on a romantic picnic while the fireworks burst overhead. How romantic could it be with someone else carrying the basket and the blanket? Tired of feeling sorry for himself, he struggled to his feet. The stitches in his side pulled. The sling on his arm made it hard to maneuver. Slow step by slow step, he shuffled around the room.

"What are you doing?" Pressley frowned, clutching papers in her hand.

"Walking. I'm going to the event tomorrow."

"No, you aren't." Her frown deepened.

"Short of being tied up, I am going. You need me to watch your back, Pressley."

"I'll ask the sheriff to have one of the deputies help me." She put her hands on his shoulders. "Please sit back down before we suffer the wrath of Mrs. White."

"Too late. You, young man, are not going to the celebration tomorrow. I'll be there manning the food tables, so I'll keep an eye on Pressley." She patted her apron pocket. "I'm packing, and I'm not afraid to use it."

"Heaven help us all." He sat down. Outnumbered or not, he would be there tomorrow. He scowled, keeping his thoughts to himself. Once they'd gone, he'd drive himself, find Pressley, and watch over her from the sidelines.

A knock sounded at the door. Mrs. White set two glasses of iced tea on the coffee table and went to let the sheriff in. "Maybe you can talk some sense into that idiot. He won't listen to me."

Sheriff Westbrook glanced from Mrs. White to River. "What did I miss?"

"He plans on going to the celebration tomorrow."

"Okay?"

She huffed. "He's in no shape to go."

"He's an adult, Mrs. White."

"Men are all fools." She stormed from the room.

"I have to agree with Mrs. White." Pressley folded her arms. "River seems to think no one can watch my back but him."

"We'll have every deputy on duty tomorrow, River. You called about emails?" He quirked a brow in Pressley's direction.

"Oh, yes." She handed the papers to him.

He scanned them. "I agree with the suspect on you leaving town for a while, but I also know it's a moot point."

"I have obligations, Sheriff."

He shrugged. "River isn't the only stubborn person in this room. We'll do our best to keep trouble away from the celebration tomorrow. Short of canceling, that's the best we can do."

"Thank you for backing me up, sir." River stood and offered his hand for a shake.

The sheriff returned the gesture. "While I stand by my opinion of you making your own decisions, you are still recovering from two gunshot wounds. Staying home might be the wisest choice. See you tomorrow, Miss Hamilton." He tipped his hat and strode from the room.

"Darn. I forgot to tell him what I found out about the love triangle." Pressley rushed from the room.

Now that no one watched, River groaned and carefully lowered himself to the sofa. Just the few steps he'd taken had worn him out. How was he going to survive an entire day tomorrow?

He stretched out and closed his eyes. When he woke up, someone had put a crocheted afghan over him. Pressley dozed in a nearby chair. The sun outside had started to set, its bright colors streaking the sky. Tonight would've been a beautiful opportunity to sit on the porch with a gorgeous woman.

When he tossed off the blanket, Pressley's eyes flew open. "You're awake."

"You didn't have to sleep in the chair, sweetheart." He sat up and rubbed his free hand over a face prickly with two days' growth of beard. "I need a shower and a shave, in that order."

"I'll call one of the hands to help you."

"No thanks. Just fill up the sink with hot water. I'll do the rest." No way would one of the hands wash him like a child.

"You're one of the most stubborn men I've ever met." Her eyes flashed. "Why don't you let someone help you?"

"I'm not an invalid." He swayed getting up from the sofa.

"You can barely stand." She rushed to his side, propping her shoulder under his unbound arm. "Please stay home tomorrow."

"No can do. I promise to bring a folding chair that I'll plop down in wherever you are. Take it or leave it."

"Ugh." Pressley helped him to the bathroom and filled the sink with hot water. She placed a rag and a bar of soap within reach. "I'll be waiting right outside. Yell if you need me."

"I'm fine." He started to close the door.

She thrust out a hand to stop him. "I want to help you, River. You'd do the same for me."

No, he'd throw her over his shoulder and take her far away from the danger coming for her.

Chapter Eighteen

River plopped a chair next to the food table, the best spot on Main Street, in his opinion, and watched as Pressley scurried here and there finalizing last-minute details before they cut the red, white, and blue streamers to let the crowd converge.

Live music, bouncy houses, and lots of food would entertain the people until the play began, which would be right before the sun set and the fireworks started. Sheriff Westbrook and his wife strolled the sidewalk opposite the diner where River sat. Other deputies took up positions to keep an eye on the partygoers. The mayor, William Thayer, carried the largest pair of scissors River had ever seen to the streamers.

River chuckled and shook his head. Such pomp and circumstance for Misty Hollow.

Cheers rang out as the mayor cut the streamers, and the crowd rushed forward.

"You behaving?" Mrs. White thrust a glass of lemonade into his hands.

"I'm sitting here doing nothing."

"Good." She patted his shoulder and moved behind the food table in order to serve the people.

"How you feeling?" Dylan and his family stopped in front of River.

River shot a quick look at Mrs. White who, thankfully, was busy serving food and gossiping. "It hurts. The arm not so much since it's in a sling, but every time I move, it's like a knife going through my side."

Dylan grinned. "I'm probably talking to the wall here, but try to stay in that chair. No two-stepping for you."

"Aw shucks, Boss. I was planning on asking Pressley to dance." He returned Dylan's grin. "Guess I'll have to be satisfied with her sitting on my lap."

"Gross." Eric took a bite out of his corn dog and ambled a few steps away.

"Yeah. Grownups are gross." Derrick copied his twin, sending the adults into fits of laughter.

"See you later." Dylan, still laughing, led his family to the bouncy houses.

Pressley, clutching a clipboard, sauntered by and tossed him a smile. Stress shadowed her eyes. Something hadn't gone according to plan, and he sat there utterly useless.

Forget it. He pushed to his feet, folded his chair, and carried it after her, despite Mrs. White's complaints trailing behind.

"What are you doing?" Pressley spun around and frowned.

"You look like you need help."

"I do. As soon as I find one of the actors, they wander off. Could you sit by the stage and prevent that from happening?"

He glanced at his watch. "The show isn't for two hours. Maybe you're herding them too soon. How about I go to the sound booth and ask them to announce that all actors should report to the stage at seven forty-five? That gives them fifteen minutes to get there."

"Okay." She stood on tiptoes and planted a quick kiss on his cheek. "Thank you. Now, go find a place to sit down. Uh-oh. Here comes Mrs. White." She laughed and hurried away.

"River Swanson." The older woman planted her hands on her hips. "What are you doing?"

"Changing locations. I'm moving to the stage."

She narrowed her eyes. "And who will make sure you stay seated all the way over there?"

"You'll just have to trust me." He chuckled and continued on his way.

"Right. Well, don't blame me if you open those stitches."

"Thank you." He raised a hand and kept going. It did feel really good to have someone mother him. He'd lost his mother years ago, and no one had stepped into the void until he'd arrived on the ranch.

The ranch had been his last resort at some semblance of life after his tour in the Middle East. Now, he had a lot of people who cared about him, including one beautiful woman named Pressley. He was a blessed man indeed.

~

Wearing sunglasses and a wig, dressed in jeans instead of coveralls, Roy stood near the portable bathrooms and watched Pressley run around Main Street like a headless chicken.

Don't worry, lady. Once the fireworks start, everything will change for you. They'd never find her where she was going. Not for a very long time at least.

Roy tore off a big bite of blue cotton candy and stuffed it in his mouth. He hadn't been able to resist spun sugar since he was a kid.

Starting to attract attention for hanging around the bathrooms too long, he strolled around the bouncy houses, occasionally standing near a kid who stood off to the side. After a few minutes, he'd move on.

When the announcement came for all actors to report to the stage, he moseyed in that direction, purchasing a glass of lemonade on his way. His stomach rumbled, but approaching the food table would put him too close to folks who might recognize him. It was best that he keep moving.

As he passed a deputy, he ducked his head and picked up the pace, falling into step with the young couple who would play the doomed lovers. Stupid idea. They'd died because of Ruby Lewis's infidelity. Why celebrate that? He grinned. The real tragedy had yet to strike. This time, the entire mine would cave in. Then, he'd step forward to purchase the land, dig through themassive piles of dirt and discover poor Pressley's bones. The town would hail him a hero.

Folks would flock to his resort to dig their own diamonds. Yeah, yeah, he'd heard people say there were no diamonds in the Duncan mine, but he believed differently. If he was wrong…so what? Folks could still dig for crystals. Either way, Roy would be a very rich man.

Maybe then he'd find a wife and have a son to carry on the family name. It would all be done legitimately this time. No bastard offspring for him.

He tossed his empty cup in a trashcan. Yep, things were going according to plan. *Watch out, Pressley. Here I come. Right along with a big bang the whole town can't miss!*

~

Pressley stood backstage as the teen boy she'd roped into volunteering moved aside the curtains so the show could start. She'd done it—turned Misty Hollow's history into something the whole town could enjoy. In a few months, she'd hopefully finish the book. Then, she could decide on her next step.

River was sitting off to the side of the stage. The poor man looked bored, but at least he was sitting still.

As the actors stepped onto the stage, tears sprang to her eyes. It seemed like the entire town had gathered to watch the thirty-minute production.

When the mine "exploded," and the curtains closed, the audience erupted in applause. Pressley took her place on the stage with the actors and bowed. The tears that had pooled in her eyes now ran down her cheeks. Finally, the town accepted her as one of their own.

"Thank you all so much for coming. Now, please, make your way to the field for the fireworks." Another bow and the curtains closed. She headed to where River sat.

An explosion behind her knocked her off her feet. Then another and another.

When the smoke cleared, she struggled to her feet as screams sounded around her. "River!" She staggered, crashing into what was left of the shattered stage.

A couple of the buildings on Main Street were

engulfed in flames. Folks lay on the sidewalk, some not moving, others bleeding.

Where was River? *God, please don't take him.*

She shoved through the stampeding crowd until she reached his empty chair. Not seeing him, she stopped and turned in a circle, trying to see through the panic that smothered Misty Hollow.

Multi-colored smoke filled the street, the kind children enjoyed from smoke bombs. Only this seemed much more ominous. This smoke was not for play; this was to kill.

Her heart hammered in her throat. Her knees stung from her fall to the asphalt. She stumbled with the crowd until she reached the food-table area. "Mrs. White!" She grabbed a napkin to press against the gash on her head.

"I'm okay. What happened?"

"The stage blew up. There are several fires burning." Her throat clogged. "I can't find River."

"No doubt he's out there helping the wounded. Pull me to my feet." She held up her hands.

Pressley helped her. "I have to find him."

"Head down Main Street. He'll be there."

If he wasn't dead or seriously wounded. "Are you sure you're all right?"

"I'm fine. Go, and, Pressley?"

"Yes?" She stopped and glanced over her shoulder.

"Be careful. This fire was no accident."

With a nod, she ignored the pain in her knees and ran down the street in search of River. She stopped several times to administer aid or help a frantic mother find her child. The frightened crowd was too thick.

She'd never find River. To get a better view, she climbed on top of a set of bleachers erected for the celebration and scanned the crowd. Spotting his dark head by the diner, she climbed down and headed in that direction. By the time she reached the diner, he was gone.

She stopped Deputy Hudson. "Have you seen River?"

"Westbrook asked him to head to the sheriff office parking lot. That's where they're taking the wounded. Lost and found is over by the drug store. Those two buildings weren't damaged by fire. Not yet anyway."

"Was he injured?"

"A few minor cuts and scrapes. Nothing like his gunshot wounds. Excuse me." He pulled free and raced away.

She changed direction for the sheriff's office.

"Ma'am, please." A woman stopped her. "I can't find my son. He's five and wearing jean shorts and a white tee shirt with a flag."

"Let's check the drugstore." Shoving aside her frantic desire to find River, she led the woman to the drugstore where a crying boy ran to her. Pressley smiled, then ran back the way she'd come.

She jumped out of the way of the fire truck, then she tripped over the curb and fell again. Tears coursed down her cheeks from her scraped palms. Her knees started to bleed into spilled popcorn kernels dotting the parking lot.

"Here, miss." A man helped her to her feet. "Let's get you to the medics."

"Thank you. That's where I was headed before

falling." She pulled back when he started to lead her in the wrong direction. Instinct had her scooping popcorn into her hand and shoving them into her pocket. "The sheriff's office is that way."

He shoved a gun into her side. "We aren't going there, Pressley. I have other plans for you. Yell for help, and I'll shoot you and whoever is close by. Nod if you understand."

Spotting a family with small children making their way past them, she nodded.

"Good girl. Now head for the diner, then the alley behind it. My truck is waiting. Act like we're friends."

Hard to do when her legs trembled so much she feared they'd collapse.

"Fall and I shoot you. Not the end I've planned, but it'll work."

"What do you have planned?"

"You know that little play you put on? How it ended onstage and after?" He laughed. "Something like that."

"You're insane. Do you realize how many people you've injured?"

"All I care about is getting what's mine. Now move faster." He jabbed her with the gun.

Though limping she stepped up her pace into the alley behind the diner where the same truck that had come upon her and River on the logging road awaited them. "You shot River."

"Too bad I didn't kill him. Move. I guarantee he'll be looking for you."

She glanced around for something to use as a weapon. If she got in that truck, she was a dead woman.

The man removed his sunglasses and aimed the

gun at her head. "Get. In. The. Truck."

She stared at the brown spot in the white of his eye. *Roy Hyatt*. Saying a prayer for safety and rescue, she climbed into the truck.

Chapter Nineteen

It took a bit of doing, but River climbed on top of the nearest vehicle and scanned the crowd for Pressley. Just as he'd spot her strawberry-blond hair, the woman would turn, and he'd see it wasn't her.

"Anything?" Ryder asked.

"No sign of her. Where did they take the wounded?"

"The sheriff department parking lot."

"Let's go."

Pressing his arm against his side to keep the pain at bay, he rushed in that direction, his friend at his side. Pressley had been near the stage when it blew up. What if she was one of the blanket-covered bodies he'd spotted in the parking lot? No. He refused to think that way. She was alive and well and looking for him. He couldn't believe otherwise.

"We'll find her." Ryder put a hand on his shoulder. "I'll get the rest of the guys—"

"Okay. I'll keep looking here. Thanks." He increased his pace as much as his wounds would allow. "Pressley Hamilton?"

"No sign of her." A medic with a clipboard riffled through some pages. "Nope. Not among the wounded or the dead."

"Is there anywhere else I could look?"

"Check the diner."." He jerked his head toward it.. "We moved it from the parking lot because we had too many everyone there."

"Thanks." He crossed the road, fighting his way through the fleeing crowd. Spotting a familiar bright redhead, he made a beeline for Lucy. "Have you seen Pressley?"

"No, but I can ask around. Wait here." She rushed to where a couple of her servers watched over lost children. A few minutes later, she returned. "She was seen heading toward the alley with a man."

His heart dropped. "What did he look like?"

"Dark hair, medium build—he could be anyone. Excuse me." She hurried to the side of a frantic woman calling out for her child.

River headed for the alley, knowing before he did that there would be no sign of Pressley. She'd been taken. After confirming his worse fear, he sprinted back to the sheriff's office. "Sheriff? Pressley was seen escorted by a man into the alley behind Lucy's. There's no sign of her."

The sheriff took a deep breath. "She'll be at the mine. Hold on while I find someone to go after her."

River couldn't wait. Once the sheriff turned, he took off for his truck at the opposite end of the street. After removing pieces of wood and other debris blown there by the explosions, he squealed tires away from the carnage of the Fourth of July celebration. He prayed he'd arrive at the mine in time to save Pressley.

He slowed his speed when heading up the mountain. Driving with one hand was tough enough without avoiding flying over the edge. He couldn't help her if he was dead.

What was her captor's objective? To kill her and then come forward as the last grieving relative, surprised to find out he had a relative living. Or had the man lost all reason? River went with the last choice—the man was far more dangerous than someone with full control over his emotions.

How much of a head start did they have? He tried to estimate how much time had passed since the explosion. An hour, at least. Had he taken her right away or waited until she was alone? River pounded the steering wheel. Why hadn't he thought to ask Lucy? Because she'd been busy caring for others.

He took a curve too sharply and forced himself to slow down until he spotted the old logging road. Every jolt over the rough surface had him gasping against the pain. His shirt stuck to his skin with blood that had seeped through his stitches. He'd worry about his wound later. *Hold on, Pressley, I'm coming.*

Stopping the truck near the spot where he'd been shot, River took a deep breath and shoved open his door. He still had a long hike ahead of him before reaching the mine. Then, tunnels to search. The futility of finding her in time threatened to consume him, stealing his breath. He would not fail her. He would find her in time. He would.

The barbed wire snagged his shirt as he crawled through, pricking the skin on his back. He gasped and continued, shoving aside thick foliage until he struggled to his feet.

Sweat poured down his back. A moonless night made vision difficult, but would have been great for the fireworks that never happened. An anticipated celebration had ended in unimaginable terror.

Now, the woman he loved had been taken. He could only pray God would lead him in the right direction.

What if the dude hadn't taken her to the mine at all? There were plenty of places on Misty Mountain for someone to disappear. No. He couldn't think that way anymore than he could think about failing her.

The two of them had a future waiting for them. One where she stayed in Misty Hollow. One where they worked together for the good of the town.

He stopped and leaned against a tree to catch his breath. Fire burned through his shoulder and side. *Come on, man. You can do this.*

He envisioned Pressley's face, tear-stained and frightened, waiting for him. She was tough—he knew that, but not even a woman as strong as Pressley could face down a cold-blooded killer alone.

"Hold on, baby, I'm coming." He pushed away from the tree and continued, swiping perspiration off his forehead with the back of his arm. River would use every last ounce of his strength—and blood if that's what it took—to save her.

~

Roy prodded Pressley through the mine opening. "Head straight, then turn right at the first opportunity."

"Didn't you already cave this place in?" She kept her steps slow and methodical, doing her best to buy time.

"There are more than one place to stash you, coz."

"River won't come. He's injured. He'll send the sheriff."

"He'll come. Cowboys always come." His words dripped derision. "Those ranch hands on the Rocking W all think they're heroes. They've come to the town's rescue on more than one occasion. Oh, yes, Swanson will come for you. Then, we'll have our own reenactment of poor fateful lovers who perish in this mine."

The man was certifiably insane. "What's so important about this land that you would kill for it? Let's sell it and split the profits."

"You'd like that, wouldn't you?"

She frowned over her shoulder, barely able to make out his features in the light of his fading flashlight. "I suggested it, didn't I?"

"Don't get smart with me. I plan on pulling my family's name from the muck and becoming something more than the handyman everyone calls on. Pick up the pace." He poked the gun in her back. "I want to have you settled before Cowboy arrives."

As injured as River was, she figured they had plenty of time. Yes, he would come for her. She wished he wouldn't, but that wasn't the type of man he was. He would do anything for the people he cared about, even risking his life.

Her throat burned from the acrid smoke. River was the type of man who would die for her. The type of man she'd looked for her entire life. Now, when she'd found him, it could all end within the recesses of a mine.

"I bet you've written bad things about the Hyatts in those notes of yours."

"Not a word. You're barely mentioned in the history of this town."

"That's what I'm going to change." He jabbed her again. "The name of Hyatt is going to be revered around here. I'm going to change this town."

"You already have by blowing up the place!" She glared back at him.

"Oh, boohoo. Nobody knows I'm the one responsible."

They would when she escaped his clutches. She'd make sure everyone knew who was responsible for the destruction. When she turned right at the first junction, Pressley subtly dropping a couple pieces of popcorn. She knew where they were. This was the tunnel she'd taken with the twins. Her hope fled when he made her turn left, then left again, but she still dropped a few kernels. Hopefully, the rodents in the mine wouldn't eat up the trail before River or the sheriff came. Any hope remaining depended on them finding the trail.

Roy laughed. "Smart girl. We want the cowboy to find you, don't we? Leave all the clues you want."

She wanted to throw her head back and headbutt him in the face. Instead, she gritted her teeth to keep from responding.

"Here we go. This is deep enough that once I blow up the entrance, no one will find you until I purchase this land, open it to the public, and voice my dismay at finding the remains of my only living relative." He chuckled. "It's the perfect plan."

She rolled her eyes and turned to face him. A meager trickle of light came from overhead, letting her know air could get in. Which meant they could get out.

"Turn back around and put your hands behind

you."

Heart in her throat, she complied. Roy secured her hands with a zip-tie. Her gaze dropped to the gym shoes she wore, and she smiled. She could get free with a bit of time. Hadn't this fool watched videos on how to escape abductors? Thank goodness she liked reading mysteries and thrillers. "You'd better hurry, Roy. Your flashlight is dying. Wouldn't want you to get lost in the mine." She grinned.

"Shut up." He dug in his pocket and pulled out some batteries. "I'm always prepared. Just like a Boy Scout. Besides, I can't leave until the cowboy arrives." He replaced the batteries, then stood against the wall.

She leaned against another dirt wall and slid to the ground. Since she didn't know what would happen after River arrived, she needed to rest and save her strength, making Roy think her compliant to his demands. As she waited, she worked at the zip-tie, doing her best to keep from grimacing when the plastic bit into her skin. Once the man left, she could use her shoestrings to cut herself loose.

She didn't know how much time had passed, only that she dozed until a soft thud jolted her awake.

Roy clicked off his flashlight, but not before she saw the satisfaction on his face. "Just as planned," he whispered.

Her heart rate increased. Her ears strained to hear more.

What sounded like a stumble. A groan.

River.

"Don't come! It's a trap." She screamed.

River stepped into view, his gaze locking on hers.

Roy clicked on his light and lunged, bringing the

butt of his weapon hard against River's head.

River dropped like a stone.

"Adios, cousin." Roy flashed another grin, macabre in the light, and raced out of sight.

Pressley pressed against the dirt wall and pushed to her feet. "River." She rushed to his side, then knelt beside him. After twisting until she maneuvered her hands in front of her, she worked at untying her shoelaces. Done, she looped one lace between her tied hands, then tied the two laces into a knot. Pedaling her feet, she sawed the lace against the zip-tie, biting back sobs as the zip-ties burned her skin. Still, she kept going as tears streamed down her face.

Focus, Pressley. You can do this. Her gaze fell on the man in front of her.

River wasn't moving. She couldn't tell if he was breathing. All she could see was the dark stain spreading across his side.

Her hands broke free.

An explosion rained rock and dirt on her head.

She threw her body over River's.

Chapter Twenty

The roof of the cave battered her body with rocks. With her body over River's, she covered her head with her arms the best she could and waited for the cave-in to end.

When it did, dust filled the air. Pressley coughed and swiped a dirty hand across her face. "River?"

He groaned in response. "What happened?"

"Roy Hyatt hit you in the head." She helped him to a sitting position. "Then, he blew up the place. We're trapped."

Blinking like an owl, he glanced around them. "Got a light?"

"Just my cell phone." She dug it from her pocket. It actually still worked. "No service, but we have light."

"Good. We'll use yours until it dies, then switch to mine." He hugged his good arm around his midsection. "Aim the light at the entrance."

She did. Her blood chilled. Rocks and beams blocked their escape. "What do we do?"

"Don't panic, Darlin'. We'll get out of here." Groaning, he struggled to his feet, using her as leverage and stopped at the blockage. "I feel air, so the entire place hasn't come down. There's an exit somewhere."

"So, we need to dig ourselves out?"

"Unfortunately." He removed a rock. "Be very careful, Pressley. If the rest of this place comes down, we're doomed. Start at the top and work your way down the middle, leaving as much at the side for support as you can. All we need is a hole big enough to crawl through."

She nodded. "Sit over there. I've got this."

"No. You can't do this alone."

"I have to, River. You're in no physical condition to help me, and you're bleeding. Please." She led him back to the wall and helped him sit. "I can do this." She turned off her light, using what little starlight seeped into the cave to see by. It wasn't much—barely more than shadows—but it was just enough. Slowly, rock by rock, she set them aside.

More and more air rushed in, cooling her perspiring skin. "You still with me, River?"

"I'm not going anywhere." His voice sounded weak to her ears. "Unless you're there."

Tears welled again. She refused to let them fall despite her fear, despite the pain in her back and shoulders. She had to be strong and get them out.

One rock at a time until she had a hole big enough for her. Then, she continued until she felt River could get through. "Come on." Propping her shoulder under his arm, she guided him to the exit. "You first. I'll hold the light and push if you get stuck."

He chuckled. "Not quite the way I envisioned you…touching me, but okay." He crawled through, twisting at one point until he fell through to the other side.

"You okay?"

"I'm good. Come on."

She scurried through, dislodging a few loose rocks, but thankfully, no more rained down on her head. Free from their prison, she aimed her light around the tunnel. "We went left, then right and right, so if we go back, turning the opposite—"

He turned toward her. "We can try, but if Roy went that way, he'll have blocked our escape."

"You should stay here. Let me find a way out and come back for you." She hated to leave him, but he didn't look as if he could stay on his feet for much longer.

"We aren't separating." He leaned against the wall.

"Listen to reason."

"I'm not going to die alone."

She gasped. "You think we're going to die?"

"We could." His features hardened. "It's reality. We stay together."

"Fine." Although her own legs threatened to give way, she let him lean on her and headed the way she thought Roy had brought her.

When they reached a blockage, they turned and headed in another direction. She tripped, taking both her and River to the dirt. Lying there, she fought to catch her breath, then aimed her light to see what she'd tripped over.

Roy, dead from a massive head wound, lay near the pile of rocks and debris.

"Looks like his plan backfired." River took a deep breath, coughed, and stood, swaying.

"If he didn't make it out, how do we think we can?" The man had known the tunnels far better than they. His dying like this was poetic justice. The world was a better place without Roy Hyatt.

"I know I sound like the bearer of bad news, but I've been wrong a lot of times." He gave her a trembling smile. "We keep going until…we can't." He held out his hand. "Together."

She grasped his. "Together."

They headed back, passing the spot where she'd dug an escape for them. "Let's follow the breeze."

"Hard to tell where it's coming from," River said.

"We know it isn't behind us." Leaning on each other, they plodded through the tunnels, sometimes so dark Pressley couldn't see her hand in front of her face. That was when the despair set in. Hope leaped anew when a flicker of light met them. Dark and light, on and on, until she began to think there was no end to the tunnels.

Once she bought the land, and she intended to, she'd make sure no one set foot in the Duncan mine ever again.

When they eventually found a way out, she planned on sleeping for a week after taking a long hot bath to soak the millions of aches and pains riddling her body. She took a deep breath and continued with River leaning more heavily on her shoulders.

~

He would not pass out. He would not fall. He would not leave Pressley to make it out alone. If he fell, she'd never leave him, and they would both perish.

"River, look." Her voice brightened. "I see the light."

Thank you, God. He forced himself to move faster.

"River? Miss Hamilton?" A light shone in their eyes and blinded them.

"Sheriff?" River's throat clogged with emotion.

"I found them! Have the medics ready." Sheriff Westbrook rushed forward and relieved Pressley of the burden of helping River. "I've got him, ma'am. Go ahead of us. There's water waiting for you."

"How did you find us?" River slowly lifted his good arm over the sheriff.

"Did you know there's actually a map of these tunnels? Had a heck of a time finding it, but we did. Just in the nick of time it appears. You look to be on your last leg."

"I feel like death warmed over, whatever that means." River locked his gaze on Pressley's back. What a remarkable woman. Beautiful, smart, and the bravest person he'd ever met. He would not have made it this far without her.

Outside, he lifted his face to the stars. A breeze blew the dust away, and he sneezed. The sneeze took him down. Now, he gazed at the stars from his back until his eyes drifted closed and darkness took over. When he opened them again, he found himself in a hospital bed. Pressley lay on top of the other bed in the room, her hands folded under her face. Rather than wake her, he stared at the woman he loved and drifted back into unconsciousness.

The next time he woke, she sat beside his bed. "Hey."

"Hey yourself." He pressed the button that raised his bed, wincing as it caused his new stitches to pull.

"We survived."

"We did." She sobered. "The sheriff sent in deputies to bring Roy's body out. It's over. Finally."

"How many died yesterday?"

"Not counting Roy…five. About twenty injured, two businesses burned down, a few others damaged—one of them being the bookstore. Sheriff Westbrook says it won't take long for the town to be back on its feet. Strong people live here. Moving on after tragedy is what they do." She took his hand and gently drew her finger around the IV needle. "You lost a lot of blood."

"I'll be okay."

She nodded, her eyes glistening. "Yes, you will."

"Sweetheart?"

She raised her face to his.

"*We* will be okay."

She nodded. 'I know."

"Good morning." Sheriff Westbrook entered the room and smiled. "How are you feeling?"

"Fine."

"Wyatt wants a full report. Says you're to take it easy for two weeks, no exceptions, and told me to lock you up if you don't obey."

"Good luck with that," Pressley said. "Short of tying him to this bed, I don't see how anyone can make him follow those orders."

"Then we'll have to turn him over to Mrs. White." The sheriff grinned.

"I promise to behave. Just don't give me over to her." River laughed, immediately regretting it again when pain shot through his side.

"The doctor said he won't be released until tomorrow, so he can't do much today." Pressley released his hand and stood. "Can I bring you coffee?"

"How are you doing, Miss Hamilton? The doctor said you've sustained quite a few bruises of your own."

"I'm stiff but doing well." She smiled at River. "Better than him by a long shot."

"Glad to hear it. I'll leave the two of you be. Come by the office when you can so we can take your statements. No rush." He tipped his hat and left them alone.

River was a fool. His first thought should've been about Pressley, but seeing her at his side…well, that had been all he needed. "Are you really doing okay?"

"Bruises will heal." She bent and planted a tender kiss on his forehead. "This looks like the only place that doesn't hurt on you."

He tapped his lips. "Here's another place."

She obliged, kissing him everywhere he said it didn't hurt. "How about that coffee? The doctor said you can have anything you want."

"Anything?" He arched a brow.

"Yes. Name it, and I'll get it, even if I have to drop into town."

He held out his hand. "Come here."

She slipped her hand into his.

"I'm going to ask for only one thing." He swallowed against a suddenly dry throat.

"Okay."

"Marry me."

Her eyes widened and filled with tears. "Really? You've only known me a couple of months."

"I know all I need to know about you, Pressley Hamilton." His lips twitched. "You did say that the doctor said I could have anything I wanted. I want you."

"I want you, too," she whispered. "More than anything."

"Sweetheart, I was yours from the moment I saw you glaring at me at the lookout point, wearing those ridiculous red heels. I'd never seen anything so beautiful in my life. Did you lose a red scarf that day?"

"Yes."

"I found it."

"You did?"

He nodded. "It's in my drawer at the bunkhouse. Found it while out riding one day."

"Why would you keep it?"

"To have something of yours in case you left Misty Hollow."

She sat back in the chair next to his bed. "I don't plan on leaving. Not ever. Yes, I'll marry you, River Swanson."

"Seal the deal with a kiss. I won't believe you otherwise."

"Greedy man."

"You have no idea."

Epilogue

Six months later

Pressley drove to the Rocking W and headed straight for the garage. She'd called earlier that day and asked River to meet her.

Since the horror of the Fourth of July, they'd spent every day together helping rebuild Main Street. Pressley had also finished her book, leaving Roy's name out. She refused to give him the satisfaction of going into the history book.

While the man's death had been horrible, his explosive going off too early, she'd hoped he would've gone to prison and received the mental help he needed. Things didn't always go according to plan though, and Roy's plan had failed him.

"Hello, beautiful." River met her at the door, drying his hands on a towel. "You really want to go to the land today?"

She nodded. "It's time. I can't stay away forever." Besides, she had a surprise for him.

"Then, let's go." He put his arm around her waist

and nuzzled her neck. "Although, I'd rather be planning our wedding."

"That's all done, silly." They were set to wed in two days. "There's something I want to do first."

"It is my mission in life to take care of all your wants." He grinned.

She gave him a playful bump with her shoulder. "You do a great job, too. I'll drive."

He shot her a questioning look but nodded.

A short time later, they stood on the edge of what had once been called Duncan land. The mine hadn't been touched since the Fourth of July. She had no intention of reopening the cursed place.

"I have something for you." She pulled a folder from the large bag she carried.

"I'm intrigued." Smiling, he opened it and studied the drawing. "What's this?"

"My vision for this land. I closed on my uncle's company and purchased this land." Her gaze locked on his. "I didn't say anything before because I wanted it to be a surprise. I'm hoping you'll be as excited as I am."

"But what is it?"

"An RV park. I'd like to widen the creek to make a fishing pond. Build a clubhouse and a playground. Make this a place people want to live. A place where they can enjoy the beauty of this mountain and forget the ugliness of what's transpired here." *Please like my idea.*

He leaned over and kissed her. "I think it's great. Never envisioned myself as anything but a mechanic, but RV park owner sounds like an adventure I'm willing to try. As long as you're at my side, I can do anything."

She stepped into his embrace. "With *The History of Misty Hollow* being published soon, I needed something else to occupy my mind. This project seems perfect and will benefit the town. Growth is always good."

"Most of the time." He chuckled. "This is far better than a tourist resort."

She shuddered. "Perish the thought. Thank you for coming for me that day." She didn't need to clarify the actual date for him.

"I can't envision a world without you in it. Either we survived or we didn't, but it would be both of us, whatever happened." He rested his chin on her head as they both stared over the land. "Where's our house going to be?"

"Over by that stand of cottonwoods. I have a drawing."

His chest rumbled under her cheek. "Of course, you do." With his forefinger, he tilted her face back to his. "I love you, Miss Smarty Pants."

"I love you." She closed her eyes, trying to think of a creative name for him, but lost herself in his kiss.

The End

www.cynthiahickey.com

Cynthia Hickey is a multi-published and best-selling author of cozy mysteries and romantic suspense. She has taught writing at many conferences and small writing retreats. She and her husband run the publishing press, Winged Publications. They live in Arizona and Arkansas, becoming snowbirds with three dogs. They have ten grandchildren who keep them busy and tell everyone they know that "Nana is a writer."

Connect with me on FaceBook
Twitter
Sign up for my newsletter and receive a free short story
www.cynthiahickey.com

Follow me on Amazon
And Bookbub
Shop my bookstore on shopify. For better price and autographed books. You can also subscribe to Mysterious Delivery, a mystery and suspense monthly book subscription with a book and several surprise goodies to pamper the reader.

Enjoy other books by Cynthia Hickey

Cowboys of Misty Hollow
Cowboy Jeopardy
Cowboy Peril
Cowboy Hazard
Cowgirl Blaze

Misty Hollow
Secrets of Misty Hollow
Deceptive Peace
Calm Surface
Lightning Never Strikes Twice
Lethal Inheritance
Bitter Isolation
Say I Don't
Christmas Stalker
Bridge to Safety
When Night Falls
A Place to Hide
Mountain Refuge

Stay in Misty Hollow for a while. Get the entire series here!

The Seven Deadly Sins series
Deadly Pride
Deadly Covet
Deadly Lust
Deadly Glutton
Deadly Envy

Deadly Sloth
Deadly Anger

The Tail Waggin' Mysteries
Cat-Eyed Witness
The Dog Who Found a Body
Troublesome Twosome
Four-Legged Suspect
Unwanted Christmas Guest
Wedding Day Cat Burglar

Brothers Steele
Sharp as Steele
Carved in Steele
Forged in Steele
Brothers Steele (All three in one)

The Brothers of Copper Pass
Wyatt's Warrant
Dirk's Defense
Stetson's Secret
Houston's Hope
Dallas's Dare
Seth's Sacrifice
Malcolm's Misunderstanding
The Brothers of Copper Pass Boxed Set

Time Travel
The Portal

Tiny House Mysteries
No Small Caper
Caper Goes Missing
Caper Finds a Clue
Caper's Dark Adventure
A Strange Game for Caper
Caper Steals Christmas
Caper Finds a Treasure
Tiny House Mysteries boxed set

Wife for Hire – Private Investigators
Saving Sarah
Lesson for Lacey
Mission for Meghan
Long Way for Lainie
Aimed at Amy
Wife for Hire (all five in one)

A Hollywood Murder
Killer Pose, book 1
Killer Snapshot, book 2
Shoot to Kill, book 3
Kodak Kill Shot, book 4
To Snap a Killer
Hollywood Murder Mysteries

Shady Acres Mysteries
Beware the Orchids, book 1
Path to Nowhere

Poison Foliage
Poinsettia Madness
Deadly Greenhouse Gases
Vine Entrapment
Shady Acres Boxed Set

CLEAN BUT GRITTY Romantic Suspense

Highland Springs

Murder Live
Say Bye to Mommy
To Breathe Again
Highland Springs Murders (all 3 in one)

Colors of Evil Series

Shades of Crimson
Coral Shadows

The Pretty Must Die Series

Ripped in Red, book 1
Pierced in Pink, book 2
Wounded in White, book 3
Worthy, The Complete Story

Lisa Paxton Mystery Series

Eenie Meenie Miny Mo

COWBOY UNCERTAINTY

Jack Be Nimble
Hickory Dickory Dock
Boxed Set

Hearts of Courage
A Heart of Valor
The Game
Suspicious Minds
After the Storm
Local Betrayal
Hearts of Courage Boxed Set

Overcoming Evil series
Mistaken Assassin
Captured Innocence
Mountain of Fear
Exposure at Sea
A Secret to Die for
Collision Course
Romantic Suspense of 5 books in 1

INSPIRATIONAL

Nosy Neighbor Series
Anything For A Mystery, Book 1
A Killer Plot, Book 2
Skin Care Can Be Murder, Book 3
Death By Baking, Book 4
Jogging Is Bad For Your Health, Book 5

Poison Bubbles, **Book 6**
A Good Party Can Kill You, **Book 7**
Nosy Neighbor collection

Christmas with Stormi Nelson

The Summer Meadows Series
Fudge-Laced Felonies, **Book 1**
Candy-Coated Secrets, **Book 2**
Chocolate-Covered Crime, **Book 3**
Maui Macadamia Madness, **Book 4**
All four novels in one collection

The River Valley Mystery Series
Deadly Neighbors, **Book 1**
Advance Notice, **Book 2**
The Librarian's Last Chapter, **Book 3**
All three novels in one collection

Historical cozy
Hazel's Quest

Historical Romances
Runaway Sue
Taming the Sheriff
Sweet Apple Blossom
A Doctor's Agreement
A Lady Maid's Honor

A Touch of Sugar
Love Over Par
Heart of the Emerald
A Sketch of Gold
Her Lonely Heart

Finding Love the Harvey Girl Way

Cooking With Love
Guiding With Love
Serving With Love
Warring With Love
All 4 in 1

Finding Love in Disaster

The Rancher's Dilemma
The Teacher's Rescue
The Soldier's Redemption

Woman of courage Series

A Love For Delicious
Ruth's Redemption
Charity's Gold Rush
Mountain Redemption
They Call Her Mrs. Sheriff
Woman of Courage series

Short Story Westerns

Flowers of the Desert

Contemporary

Romance in Paradise
<u>Maui Magic</u>
<u>Sunset Kisses</u>
<u>Deep Sea Love</u>
<u>3 in 1</u>

<u>Finding a Way Home</u>
<u>Service of Love</u>
<u>Hillbilly Cinderella</u>
<u>Unraveling Love</u>
<u>I'd Rather Kiss My Horse</u>

Christmas
<u>Dear Jillian</u>
<u>Romancing the Fabulous Cooper Brothers</u>
<u>Handcarved Christmas</u>
<u>The Payback Bride</u>
<u>Curtain Calls and Christmas Wishes</u>
<u>Christmas Gold</u>
<u>A Christmas Stamp</u>
<u>Snowflake Kisses</u>
<u>Merry's Secret Santa</u>
<u>A Christmas Deception</u>

The Red Hat's Club (Contemporary novellas)

<u>Finally</u>

Suddenly
Surprisingly
The Red Hat's Club 3 – in 1

Short Story

One Hour (A short story thriller)
Whisper Sweet Nothings (a Valentine short romance)

www.ingramcontent.com/pod-product-compliance
Lightning Source LLC
Chambersburg PA
CBHW070423310726
48977CB00003B/814